Garnet

The Widows of Wildcat Ridge Series
Book 9

Caroline Clemmons

CAROLINE CLEMMONS

Garnet
The Widows of Wildcat Ridge Series
Book 9
By
Caroline Clemmons

ISBN: 9781793977472

Copyright © 2018 by Caroline Clemmons

Cover © Charlene Raddon, silversagebookcovers.com

All rights reserved. Without limiting the rights under copyright reserved above, no part of this publication may be reproduced, stored in or introduced into a retrieval system or transmitted in any form or by any means (electronic, mechanical, photocopying, recording, or otherwise) without the prior written permission of the copyright owner.

Names, characters, places, and incidents are either the product of the author's imagination or are used fictitiously. Any resemblance to actual persons living or dead, businesses, events, or locales is purely coincidental.

GARNET

Table of Contents

Chapter One 5
Chapter Two 11
Chapter Three 19
Chapter Four 25
Chapter Five 30
Chapter Six 35
Chapter Seven 39
Chapter Eight 43
Chapter Nine 47
Chapter Ten 53
Chapter Eleven 58
Chapter Twelve 65
Chapter Thirteen 69
Chapter Fourteen 73
Chapter Fifteen 77
Chapter Sixteen 81
Chapter Seventeen 85
Chapter Eighteen 90
Chapter Nineteen 94
Chapter Twenty 99
Chapter Twenty-One 105
Chapter Twenty Two 109
Chapter Twenty Three 114
Chapter Twenty Four 118
Chapter Twenty Five 122
Epilogue 126
About Caroline Clemmons 134

DESERET NEWS
Salt Lake City, Utah

Est. 1831 Monday, March 31, 1884 Price 10¢

Disaster Strikes Gold King Mine

On Friday, March 28, an explosion and fire in the Gold King Mine, Wildcat Ridge, Utah, resulted in a total collapse, killing an estimated 143 miners. Mine owner, Mortimer Crane, says the disaster occurred during the shift change, with men from both shifts being killed. As townspeople attempted to rescue survivors, a second explosion raised the death toll to approximately 175.

Crane states it is impossible to tell now exactly what caused the first explosion and fire or the second explosion. The violence of the blast and faulty shoring is said to have likely caused the lower levels to collapse. Local physician, Dr. Josiah Spense, reported most victims died quickly of suffocation.

Witnesses report that the collapse and explosion were felt as far as thirty miles away. Minor landslides occurred, windows broken and buildings damaged.

Retrieving all the bodies was impossible but a mass burial of those recovered is planned for April 12 at the Wildcat Ridge Cemetery. Anyone wishing to aid the widows and the children left fatherless by the catastrophe may send donations to the Wildcat Ridge Post Office in envelopes marked Donation.

GARNET

Chapter One

September 1884
Wildcat Ridge, Utah Territory

Garnet Chandler startled awake. Who was in her bedroom? She fought to keep from gasping aloud. While she lay frozen, her heart pounded. She'd almost called out to see if her niece or nephew was there. Neither child would creep around the room instead of speaking her name and crawling onto her bed.

Light from the almost full moon shone through the window and outlined an adult moving with stealth. She was certain she watched a man whose wiry shape, hunched shoulders, and prominent Adam's apple reminded her of someone.

A dresser drawer glided open with barely a scrape. Why would anyone sneak about her room? What if this person hurt her niece and nephew? She couldn't allow this intruder to violate the sanctity of her home.

Her hand slid under her pillow and grasped her late husband's Colt .45. Without a rustle, she aimed at the shadow. She fought to keep fear from altering her voice.

"Stop and raise your hands or I'll shoot."

The unwanted visitor tossed a drawer at her and ran from the room. No longer trying for silence, he clomped down the stairs and out the café's back door. Hands shaking, she rose from bed, grabbed her robe, and slid her feet into felt slippers.

How had he gained entry? She shoved the revolver into her robe's pocket and rushed to check on her niece. The lamp burning low in the child's room provided a soft glow.

The six-year-old sat up in bed, clutching her favorite doll to her chest. "What was that noise? Molly and I were scared."

"Nothing to worry about, Hyacinth, a drawer fell on the floor. Go back to sleep, dear." She kissed Hyacinth's golden curls and tucked the cover around her and her doll.

As she left her niece's room, she discovered her nephew standing in the hall. Joey clutched a thick stick that looked like the handle from an axe or a pick.

She put a finger to her lips and nodded toward Hyacinth's room.

He whispered, "I saw a man run down the stairs."

She guided him toward his room. "Hyacinth stays so frightened I didn't want her to know. I'm going to check the door and window locks downstairs."

Joey fell in step with her. "I'm coming too. Let's take my lamp."

Since their parents' death, both children required frequent reassurance they were safe. Usually the two slept with a lamp lit and the wick turned low. She didn't mind since the light helped dispel their fear.

Her eight-year-old nephew tried hard to be the man of the family. His parents and her husband had died in the mine disaster several months ago. Since then, the children had lived with her.

She kept her hand in her pocket on the revolver as she crept down the stairs. The back door stood ajar.

"The lock is broken."

How had someone managed to destroy the lock without waking her? She was so exhausted from operating the café on her own. Perhaps she'd slept too soundly to hear the noise.

Garnet closed the door and scooted the pie safe against it. Flimsy protection at best but she couldn't do better tonight. From the position of the moon, she judged the time to be past midnight.

She checked both kitchen windows and they were locked. So were the front door and the front windows. Her nephew kept close to her while she patrolled.

"What are we gonna do?" Joey asked.

"I'll get a blanket and a pillow and sleep down here tonight. Tomorrow, I'll report the break in to Marshal Wentz and get someone to repair the door latch. Thank you for your help, but now you need to go back to bed and sleep."

"I'll stay here with you."

"Growing boys need a lot of sleep. Come on and I'll tuck you in." She ruffled his sandy-colored hair. "Don't roll your eyes at me. You're not too grown up to have me tuck you in at night."

"Okay-y-y." He shuffled up the steps. In his room, he sat on the bed and looked at his lamp. "Reckon you could leave a light on a little brighter, just for tonight?"

"Of course." She adjusted the lamp's wick. If doing so would helped reassure him, he could have two lamps burning all night. He tried to be brave but he was still an eight-year-old child.

"Now, under the cover." When she'd tucked him in, she kissed his forehead.

Since the death of the children's parents and her husband, she'd left a lamp burning for each child. Many nights, Hyacinth and Joey would wander into her room rather than sleep alone. She had to admit their presence had helped her sleep.

She missed Michael's companionship. She also missed his brother, Josiah, and sister-in-law, Dessie. Dessie had become her best friend.

Carrying a blanket and a pillow, she went to the kitchen. A cot was in the storeroom. She brought it out and put the narrow bed against the pie safe. If anyone tried to enter, they'd wake her.

Tomorrow would be busy so she needed her rest. She plopped onto the cot and tried to sleep. The revolver went back under her pillow.

Her fear magnified every noise. She was certain she would have heard a moth's wings in her current state. Not only her safety was involved, she had two orphans to protect. How she loved those two sweet children left in her care.

Near daylight, she rose and went to her room to dress. She had managed to doze on and off but exhaustion weighed down her body. She felt many times as old as her twenty-one years.

Every day since the disaster had added to her fatigue. The pressure of being on her own while providing for two children gnawed away at her. One thing was for certain, she needed help running this café.

After she'd dressed, she restored her room. The drawer her housebreaker had thrown was one in which she'd kept important papers. Now they were scattered across the room and the drawer had cracked.

She picked it up and set it aside before restoring order. Perhaps the drawer could be mended. She wondered if the blacksmith or the undertaker would accept the job.

By the time the children came down, she'd set their food and hers on the family table in the kitchen. When they'd finished, she got meat frying, biscuits in the oven, and was soon ready to open for breakfast.

"Whose turn is it to turn the sign today?"

Hyacinth leaped from her chair. "Mine." The child rushed to the front and turned the *Closed* sign to *Open* then unlocked the front door.

Fortunately, Marshal Cordelia Wentz was the first person to arrive.

Garnet spoke quietly. "Woke up to a prowler in my room last night. Ruined the lock on the back door."

"I'd better see. You go ahead with your business. Joey can show me before he goes to school." Cordelia strode through the swinging door into the kitchen.

Garnet had no choice but to let her nephew be the marshal's guide. Hungry people wanted their food in a timely manner. She had no intention of turning away paying customers. After almost no business due to the mine disaster, she was finally seeing an increase in customers.

Cordelia was soon back. "Joey said the man ran down the stairs and out to the alley. You recognize him?"

Garnet described the outline she'd seen. "I have a creepy feeling, as if I should know who he was. For the life of me, I can't figure who he could be."

GARNET

"I'll keep a lookout for the description you gave me, but that fits half the men in the county. You let me know if you see anyone suspicious hanging around."

Garnet hurried from the dining room carrying dirty dishes to the kitchen then back to the dining room laden with plates of hot food. In between, she poured what seemed like gallons of coffee. She was run off her feet until the breakfast rush slowed. Not for the first time since his death, she was grateful for Mike's extravagance in purchasing so many dishes.

Around ten, she was happy to see her friend come into the café.

Rosemary Brennan took a seat. "I stopped by for a cup of coffee and friendly conversation."

Garnet poured two cups of coffee. She set leftover biscuits, jam, and butter on the table for each of them. "I'm always happy to see you—and happy for a chance to sit down."

"Mmm, your biscuits are so fluffy." She twirled her knife at Garnet. "You know, though, I wish you would make those sticky buns like Dessie used to make. Those were so good."

Garnet took a sip of coffee. "Everyone loves them but they take extra time I simply don't have. I haven't made them since the horse auction."

"Aww, and I missed getting one then. You had Ailsa McNair helping you, didn't you?"

"And her daughter, Tillie, but that was just for the one event. I can't afford to hire anyone permanently."

Her friend leaned forward. "Garnet, you'll have to employ someone at least part time. You look totally exhausted."

Garnet grimaced and brushed a stray lock of hair from her eyes. "Truthfully, I'm so tired I can't think straight. Getting everything done on my own is almost impossible. Sometimes I think I could go to bed, pull the covers over my head, and sleep for a week."

Rosemary spread jam on a second biscuit. "My dear friend, you can't let yourself get sick with two children depending on you."

"You're right. I couldn't love those two more if I'd given birth to them. They're my precious treasures and the reason I can continue working so hard."

A wide smile graced Rosemary's lovely face. "They do seem to be especially good children. Even so, they're a new responsibility that's adding to your mental and physical strain."

"That's not what's worrying me today." She told her friend about the prowler the previous evening.

Rosemary clasped Garnet's hand. "Oh, Garnet, that must have been so frightening. I hope whoever he was doesn't return. You need help here to discourage that sort of thing from happening."

Garnet's finger traced the fluer de lis pattern on the oiled cloth that covered the table. "I know I have to do something. If only I had someone to do the heavier chores. Michael used to lift the heavy pots of liquid and sacks of flour and so forth and watch the range to make certain nothing burned while I was in the dining room."

Rosemary pushed away from the table. "I hope you think of something before your health is ruined. Sorry, I don't mean to sound so sour. Guess I've let being upset with Miles color my mood."

Recognizing the pain in her friend's voice, Garnet rose and hugged Rosemary's shoulders. "Give him the benefit of the doubt. You'll see, he'll return and you can work out your misunderstanding."

"I pray you're right." Rosemary returned the hug then left.

Garnet carried their plates and cups to the kitchen where a giant mound of dirty dishes awaited

GARNET

Chapter Two

Adam Bennett blinked awake and fought to remember where he was. Slowly the unpleasant memories returned. The beating and robbery. Being kicked into the ravine.

He waved his arms at the crows gathered in the trees overhead. He was grateful for the brush that had protected him from the birds. He staggered to his feet and braced against a tree.

How long had he been unconscious?

Tentatively, he touched the knot on his forehead. From the way the spot hurt, he'd expected it to be big as an orange. Instead, it was pecan-sized. The other bruises he'd collected in the fight and on the painful fall into the ravine hurt like a son-of-a-gun.

Worse, he felt like a green tinhorn for letting Frank Lawson and his two pals get the drop on him. Frank had kicked him so hard Adam had rolled into the gorge before the trio were finished punching him. Adam gave thanks for that.

As he'd careened down the ravine's side, one of the men had yelled at Frank, "Hey, I wanted those boots."

The other man cried, "And, I wanted his coat."

Frank's anger carried in his voice, "Then go get 'em."

Lucky for Adam, they hadn't checked to see if he was dead. Otherwise, he would be. Bad enough they stripped him of his gear plus stole his horse and pack mule.

The descent was painful and fast. Near the bottom, he'd managed to roll under a stand of brush. He hoped he was out of sight in case they decided to use him for target practice. After that, he'd passed out.

He wasn't giving up until he had that killer Lawson back in prison and on the way to the gallows. Fancy talk for a man without a penny to his name, no food, no water, who was afoot, injured—and who was near the bottom of a deep ravine. In addition, he was covered in mud, twigs, leaves, and who knew what else. Things weren't looking good, but at least he wasn't dead.

After testing his legs and wobbling to his knees, he found a lengthy branch. He used his knife to fashion it into a crutch-like walking stick. Rocks of all sizes and deadwood from tree trunks to twigs littered the ravine's sandy base. The road above him was too steep a climb for now.

He'd been traveling a half hour when he spotted tracks of a wildcat headed the same direction as he was. This time of day he doubted a cat would be on the prowl. He sure didn't want to risk being wrong.

His stick would be no defense against an angry wildcat. He didn't want one close enough he could use his knife or the small gun in his boot. At least having the two weapons gave him some comfort.

Looking up toward the trail sent his head pounding worse and the world around him spinning. He leaned against a tree trunk and tried again. Searching above and forward of him, he spotted a place where he might handle the ascent.

Climbing was almost beyond his capability in his battered condition. He fell and skidded down on his stomach. He tried again, fell, but didn't slide down as far this time.

The palms of his hands now matched the knuckles bruised and skinned from defending himself. He'd never been so filthy. He wasn't sure but he thought that was blood staining the knees of his britches.

On his third try he reached the road and rested on the trunk of a dead tree. When he'd recovered enough to go on, the way was downhill. Unless he'd totally lost his bearings, the town in the little valley below was Wildcat Ridge. Likely Lawson and his two cohorts were holed up near or in the town.

By the time he hobbled to Wildcat Ridge's outskirts, dark had settled in. That was fine with him. If Lawson and his two friends were here, Adam didn't want them to know he'd survived. First, he needed a place to recover.

A brisk wind swept down from the mountain to remind him he needed shelter soon. He didn't need a reminder to know he needed food. If he had, the rumbles of his stomach would have served.

GARNET

Still carrying his walking stick, he crept from shadow to shadow. Some of the houses appeared vacant. He didn't dare check in case Lawson and his two henchmen might be camped in one. He was in no shape to meet those three now. Besides, he sure would appreciate some food.

Crystal Café caught his attention. The place appeared to be closed but light shone around the door from the dining room into the kitchen. He went to the back door. Sure enough, a lamp burned inside. Someone moving inside cast a shadow on the closed window curtains.

***

Garnet had cleaned the mess made from today's meals, helped the children with their school lessons, fed them and herself, and was organizing for the next day. Hyacinth and Joey played checkers at the kitchen table.

Hyacinth clapped her hands. "Garnet, did you see? I won."

"Congratulations, dear." Garnet smiled at Joey, such a good boy. He made certain his sister won often enough to keep her interested.

A loud rap at the back door startled her. Because she kept the curtains closed unless they were serving food she couldn't see who had knocked.

Joey grabbed his stick. "Don't answer it. Might be the robber there."

She wiped her hands on her apron. "Or a friend who needs something." Joey didn't know the Colt was in her apron pocket. After taking a deep, bracing breath and sliding her hand around the Colt, she opened the door.

The dirtiest man she'd ever seen stood there. His beard was as dirty as his clothes. Fresh cuts and bruises showed through the mud on his face. He was tall and broad-shouldered but looked as if he could barely stand.

"Ma'am, my name is Adam Bennett. Please don't be put off by my appearance. I was robbed up the mountain a ways and lost all my gear. I'm mighty hungry. If you need anything done, I like to work for a meal."

Joey was by her side. "He isn't the one from last night." All the same, her nephew kept his pick handle in his hand.

"We're the Chandlers. Come in and sit down. Wait, wash your hands and face at the sink first. You can't handle food while you're that filthy."

While the man washed his hands, she filled a plate from leftovers and poured a cup of coffee. "Joey, please get my medicine box from upstairs."

He leaned close. "I don't think I should leave you alone while he's here."

Joey took being man of the family seriously. She humored him. "Oh, all right. Hyacinth, would you get the medicine box for me?"

"How come he doesn't have to and I do?" Usually sweet, Hyacinth was a bit spoiled and definitely jealous of her brother."

"Because Mr. Bennett is injured and needs our help. Please hurry."

Her niece stomped up the stairs while muttering under her breath, her golden curls bouncing with each step.

When Garnet glanced at the man, she saw he'd wolfed down his food. "I'll get you more. How long since you've eaten?"

"Not sure how long I was in and out of consciousness up there. They attacked me on Saturday morning. Is this still Saturday?"

"Monday. No wonder you're hungry." She set another plate of food in front of him and refilled his cup.

Hyacinth returned with Garnet's medicines. "This is awful heavy. I should get a treat for carrying this big, heavy box down the stairs all by myself."

Garnet opened the container and extracted several jars. She stopped long enough to plant a kiss on her niece's cheek. "You've had enough treats for today. Help your brother put away the checkers and your school work so you can get ready for bed."

After examining the man's face, she soaked a piece of cotton wool in weak carbolic acid solution and gently cleaned the scrapes and bruises. "That's quite a knot on your forehead. You probably have a concussion. Perhaps I should send for the doctor."

GARNET

He grinned around a split lip. "Naw, impossible to dent this hard head. I'll be fine now that I've had some food. What can I do to repay you?"

A ridiculous plan circled in Garnet's mind. She agreed with Joey that this was not last night's prowler. He could be a partner of the man who'd broken in but she didn't sense that he was. If Mr. Bennett were here, perhaps the thief wouldn't return.

Had she lost her mind?

She filled a pan with warm, soapy water and set it for him to soak his hands. "I need help here. If you're going to be in town for a while, would you be able to help me in the kitchen? That would give you time to heal from the beating."

Surprise registered on his face. "Reckon I can. What did your boy mean when he said I wasn't the one from last night?"

She glanced at Hyacinth. In case Miss Priss was listening, she lowered her voice. "Someone ruined the door's lock last night and came upstairs. I woke with him in my room, going through my things. When I challenged him to stop or I'd shoot, he threw a drawer at me and ran. By the time I donned my robe and slippers he'd run out the door."

"Any damage except the lock?"

"Other than frightening my nephew and me, he cracked the drawer of a nice piece of furniture." The thought of what might have happened sent dread through her. "Considering all the other possibilities, I suppose that's minor."

He nodded toward her niece and nephew. "So these children aren't yours?"

"No, my husband and their parents were killed when the mine exploded a few months ago. Dessie, the children's mother, helped me here during busy times. Josiah…Joe, their father, was a miner. My husband helped in the café, especially with the heavy lifting. I'm having difficulty stretching to sole café employee and new mother while still grieving."

Joey tugged at her sleeve. "You 'member our plan?"

"I have things ready to set out. Don't worry, I'll do as we discussed." She kissed the top of his head. "Now, put your sister to bed, will you? I'll be busy here for a while longer."

Looking embarrassed, he glanced at Adam before he turned back to her and whispered, "Can I leave the lamp burning bright?"

"Yes, I think that will be best." She kissed Hyacinth's cheek. "Let Joey tuck you in tonight."

Hyacinth leaned into Garnet. "I s'pose it's okay. I like it better when you read to us before you hear our prayers."

Garnet hugged the girl. "I like that best, too, dear, but I have things to do in the kitchen after I get Mr. Bennett settled. Perhaps Joey will tell you a story if you're good."

When the children had gone upstairs, Garnet gestured to the pie safe. "I moved this against the door last night then put the cot up against it."

He rose from his chair. "The lock's mended?"

"Yes, the marshal sent someone."

"I'd like to talk to your marshal."

"If you don't mind waiting until morning, she'll be one of the first to arrive for breakfast."

Surprise spread across his face. "Your marshal is a woman?"

"Surely you've heard about our mine disaster. We had many widows left here." She rested a hand at her throat, the memories creating sadness.

She pulled herself from her reverie with a deep breath. "The remaining miners moved to another mine. A lot of people moved on west or returned to their former homes. Most of the town offices are now held by women."

A frown creased his brow. "You think the town will survive after losing so many?"

"Yes, in fact new people have moved in already. A few of the widows have remarried. Others—like me—have discovered ways to keep their businesses going."

"I'm mighty grateful for the grub. You serious about me staying here?"

GARNET

"There's a cot in the storeroom. There's only a tiny window near the ceiling for fresh air but if you leave the door open perhaps you won't mind. A cot's not comfortable for as large a man as yourself but you'll have privacy."

"Ma'am, as tired as I am I could fall asleep on a bed of rocks. I barely made it to your door."

"I'm sorry for you trouble. If staying here is agreeable to you, you can go ahead and turn in. I haven't had a good night's sleep since my husband was killed on March 28th. With you asleep in there to keep anyone from breaking in, then I can finally relax and get a decent night's rest." She carried a stack of tin cans to the stairs and lined them up on the steps.

He watched her but didn't offer his help. "I'm not the nicest person you'll ever meet but I'm an honorable man. All the same, I think your friends would tell you not to trust someone you don't know—especially in my current filthy state."

When she'd added another load of cans, she stood back to admire her work. "They probably would, but they have their own problems and I'll take care of mine. I'll warn you I sleep with a Colt .45 and I know how to use it. I imagine you have a boot gun or knife or both."

His blue eyes sparkled with humor. "How did you guess?"

She shrugged. "I can't explain why, I just thought you would." She nodded at the steps. "This is Joey's and my idea to prevent the prowler from getting upstairs without us hearing. Even though you're here, I promised him I'd remember our plan."

"Good idea in case I sleep too sound. Those are sure to raise a ruckus if someone goes up in the dark."

When he stood and removed his coat, his shirt was almost as muddy as the outer garment. He draped the coat over the back of a chair and stood then shifted from one foot to the other. Something bothered him but he hesitated to mention it.

Realization hit her. "Since you don't want those who attacked you to know you're here, you should use the chamber pot that's in the store room instead of going out back to the privy." She wasn't crazy enough to invite him to use the bathing room upstairs.

She lit another lamp and gave it to him. "You'll need this."

"Thank you. I don't want the three who beat me to know I'm alive until I've recovered. As you suggested, I'll stay here in the kitchen and storeroom so no one will see me."

"I'll tell the marshal but no one else needs to know about your presence until you're ready."

GARNET

Chapter Three

A din as loud as a brass band woke Garnet. She shoved her feet into her slippers and pulled on her robe as she sped from her room. Hyacinth and Joey stood in the hallway. Her niece was cowed behind Joey and crying.

Garnet hugged Hyacinth. "Everything is all right, dear. Stay up here with your brother."

Joey hefted his pick handle. "He came back but the cans worked."

"You wait here while I investigate." She hoped Adam Bennett was all right.

When she rounded the corner so she could see the kitchen, he'd lighted the lamp. Holding it aloft, he stood at the open back door. She rushed down the stairs, avoiding the tin cans still on the steps and those scattered across the floor.

He looked up. "Reckon he picked the lock this time. It's not broken." He closed and secured the door.

"Are you okay?"

He held up a piece of cloth. "That I am but I failed to capture your visitor. Tore off this piece of his shirt as he escaped."

He examined the fabric near the lamp. "Well, I'll be."

"Something special about the fabric?"

"Matter of fact, this is from a shirt of mine that was in the gear they stole."

"How can you be sure?" She stared at the piece of material.

He held it so she could get a closer look. "See here where I sewed a tear? I can sew on a button but I'm not much of a hand with a needle and only have white thread. This was a new shirt so I tried to repair the rip. Looks like this tore right along the mended part." Indeed, pieces of white thread dangled from the edge of the red plaid scrap.

"So, now you know who the prowler is."

He gave a slight nod. "Frank Lawson."

Garnet staggered backward and grasped the newel post support. "F-Frank? N-No, no, no, that can't be. He's in prison."

Adam grasped her shoulders. "Hey, steady. Obviously you know him."

He guided her toward the kitchen table. "Sorry to spring the news on you but I had no idea you knew the man. He killed a guard breaking out of prison. Later, he shot my friend to get two horses."

Without his help she would have fallen. She made it to a chair and plopped onto the seat before her knees gave way. The room spun around her. Her stomach roiled and she thought she might throw up or lose consciousness.

He pushed her head between her knees. "Deep breaths." Kneeling in front of her, he asked, "You gonna be all right now?"

No, she wasn't even close. Instead, she was terrified. "How can I be? Even your mentioning his name scared me out of my wits."

She considered the possibility with growing dread. "I suppose him being the prowler makes sense. He's a second cousin and he's always been crazy mean." She tried to tighten her robe's tie but her hands trembled too much.

He knelt in front of her. "What's he after?"

"He thought because he's a couple of years older than me that my grandmother's jewelry should go to him. Granny was adamant when she gave all of it to me."

"Her possessions to do with as she saw fit."

"Frank didn't agree. I'm named Garnet after Granny, you see, and she was named after her mother and grandmother. There're numerous pieces including garnet necklaces, ear bobs, hair combs, brooches, and bracelets."

"Guess missing out on that much upset him."

The memory of Frank's rage sent shivers through her. "He was so angry I thought he was going to kill Granny and me right then. My uncle arrived and calmed Frank. Less than half an hour later, he was arrested for killing a man. I suspect he'd killed others as well but didn't get caught."

GARNET

Adam Bennett pulled a chair facing hers and eased onto it. "Are you talking valuable jewelry?"

She shook her head then regretted the motion. "Probably not. You see, they're garnets, not rubies. Well, I suppose the stones around them could be real diamonds. And, of course there's the gold used in the settings and chains."

"Have you had them appraised?"

"No need. Their value to me is that they're family heirlooms that go back five generations."

"Having them appraised would let you insure them."

"I hadn't considered that. I love knowing that I'll be able to pass them on—to Hyacinth and Joey if I don't have children. I'm sure Frank would sell the jewelry—or use them as a stake at poker or faro."

His expression was solemn as he met her gaze. "Mrs. Chandler, if he wants those jewels, he won't stop until he has them or he's been captured. Can you lock the gems in the bank safe?"

She pressed a hand to her aching forehead. "I suppose I could. What's to stop him from robbing the bank?"

"Reckon your marshal and I would try. Robbing the bank would be harder than stealing them from you. Regardless, you and the children wouldn't be in danger."

"Why were you after Frank? Are you a lawman?"

He shook his head then looked at his hands. "Bounty hunter. There's a five hundred dollar price on Lawson's head. A hundred each on his friends."

"That's a lot of money." She shook her head slowly. "Not worth dying for, though."

Rising to his feet, he paced the room. "I don't intend to die."

Her gaze followed him. "You didn't plan on him stealing your gear and animals."

He paused and shrugged. "You're right, I didn't intend to let him to get the drop on me. Believe me, I won't let that happen again."

To her, his plan was foolhardy. "The odds are still three to one."

"I'll have to even the odds. I need to talk to your marshal. You said she'd be here in the morning."

"She usually comes for breakfast. If she doesn't, I'll send Joey for her."

He shrugged again. "We might as well go back to sleep. He won't be back tonight."

She headed for the stairs. "Goodnight, Mr. Bennett. Thank you for your help."

***

After the beautiful Mrs. Chandler had gone upstairs, Adam used a lantern to look at the downstairs. The kitchen was large with the fanciest range he'd ever seen. It had two water reservoirs to keep hot water available. Handy in a kitchen.

On closer look, pipes from one reservoir went into the wall. He figured it went upstairs to a bathing room. A tub of hot water would sure feel good about now.

Cupboards on two sides held more dishes than a fancy hotel would use. The stairs took up part of one wall and the storeroom opened under those. The table and chairs looked as if they were used only for the family. The usual pie safes and cabinets must be handy.

He carried a lantern through the swinging door to the dining room. Man, he couldn't believe his eyes. Two fancy glass chandeliers hung from the ceiling. The tables in here were covered by oiled cloth instead of the white linen that would have gone better with the fancy light fixtures.

Someone sure spent a lot decorating this place. Better suited to Denver or St. Louis. Shaking his head slightly, he went back to the storeroom.

***

The next morning, Garnet gathered articles of her husband's clothing to take to Mr. Bennett, who she thought of as Adam. She found him sweeping the kitchen.

"My husband was a little shorter than you and not quite as muscular, but these clothes are clean."

Adam leaned the broom against the wall to take the clothing. "I'll be happy to have less mud on me. I've slapped at the grime, but still I leave a gritty trail wherever I walk."

GARNET

She chuckled. "I'd noticed, but it's not your fault, Mr. Bennett."

"Please, call me Adam or Bennett, no mister involved."

"Thank you. As I mentioned, my name is Garnet."

He shook his head. "I'll call you Mrs. Chandler. Don't want any talk arising."

"That's considerate and gentlemanly but there's no danger of gossip. At least, not from anyone who matters. I'm afraid we widows have had to make so many concessions to our circumstances that many forms of propriety have been discarded. While we're all honorable women, we simply can't dwell on the way we used to live. Each of us is trying our best simply to survive."

He dropped the bundle of clothing she'd given him and failed to catch it. "But you said there are new people in town and that the town won't die."

"That's true, but that doesn't mean each of us will be successful in holding on to our business. I believe I can keep the café going if things continue as they have the past couple of months. Another disaster could change that."

He bent to gather up the clean duds. "Reckon we'd better do our best to make sure Lawson isn't that disaster. He came here for a reason. Other than your family jewelry, what else would bring him to this town?"

"There's the new gold mine. The assay office is back in business and so is Wells Fargo, complete with a bank. In fact, my friend Grace and her husband Ben operate the Wells Fargo office."

"Then that's where you should take your heirlooms." His baritone voice was firm, as if he was used to giving orders and having them obeyed.

His bossiness irritated her. She didn't intend to take orders from a stranger down on his luck. "I don't know, Adam. I don't want my friends to be endangered or robbed either."

"That's their job, not yours. I'm sure they have a sturdy safe. Besides, you have two children to consider."

He'd brought up her weakness—the children. With a sigh, she acquiesced. "Of course you're right, I'm responsible for their welfare."

She clasped her hands at her breast. "I'd die if anything happened to Hyacinth or Joey. They're wonderful children I love and my only family."

"So, tomorrow, you'll take that jewelry to the bank?"

Why did she feel defeated? "Yes, I will as soon as the noon rush is over."

GARNET

Chapter Four

Adam had an apron tied around his waist and was stirring potatoes and onions in a skillet when a woman wearing a badge entered from the dining room. A man who also wore a badge accompanied her.

"You must be the marshal, the very person I needed to see." The britches he wore stopped above his ankles and the shirt sleeves ended above his wrists. At least they were clean, but he must look like a kid who'd outgrown his clothes.

"I am indeed Marshal Cordelia Wentz. Garnet said your name is Adam Bennett." Cordelia gestured to the man beside her. "This is County Sheriff Aubrey Bowles. He'll be interested in hearing about what happened here."

Adam shook the sheriff's hand. "The prowler returned last night but got away again. However, this time I know who he is." He proceeded to tell them about Frank Lawson and his connection to Garnet Chandler.

He reached over to the next skillet and turned the ham slices while he kept the potatoes and onions browning. "Since he wants the jewelry Mrs. Chandler has, I've advised her to take it to Wells Fargo and have the gems locked in their safe. Perhaps that will redirect Lawson's attempt to steal them."

Cordelia assessed Adam. "How are you recovering from that beating?"

He felt a flush travel across his neck and face. "Good food and a night's rest indoors has me feeling much better. I confess I'm still no match for those three. I managed to surprise Lawson last night or I'd never have been able to tackle him. He's wiry but surprisingly strong. I'm embarrassed to admit he got away."

The sheriff nodded. "From what I've heard, Lawson's also vicious and doesn't like to leave witnesses who could identify him. You're lucky to be alive."

Adam scooped the potatoes into a large bowl and set it on the warming shelf. "Believe me, I'm aware of that fact. If I hadn't fallen down the ravine, I'd be dead for certain." He chuckled. "As it turns out, I'm only halfway there."

Garnet—he called her Mrs. Chandler but thought of her by her given name—came in and helped several plates. "Thank you for keeping things going in here, Adam. Have you explained everything to the marshal and sheriff?"

He grinned at her. "I've been telling them of my exciting escapades."

She loaded the filled plates on her arms. "Cordelia, Aubrey, thanks for talking to Adam. I've been worrying about this but now I feel better." Before anyone could answer, she pushed through the swinging door into the dining room.

Cordelia met his gaze. "You joke about your fate, and that says a lot about you. I take it you're staying on to help Garnet for a while?"

"Mrs. Chandler asked me to help with the heavy work while I'm healing. You can see she needs someone else here."

Joey looked up from the table. His wide eyes carried sadness and worry. "I help all I can."

Adam turned toward the boy. "I know you do, Joey. Your aunt told me what a big help you are. The thing is, she needs an adult here while you're in school. I guess that's me for a while."

The boy's expression showed his relief. "Soon we won't have school 'til spring 'cause of the snow. Then I can help all the time."

Adam turned back to the marshal. "Does that mean people won't come to the café during the bad weather?"

She grimaced. "Not as many, but the customers who live in town will come here. She doesn't serve supper during the winter, just breakfast and lunch."

"So, her income will really decrease. That's too bad."

The marshal shook her head. "Garnet's a good businesswoman and I'm sure she's going to be all right. In fact, I think most people in town are recovering from the disaster if Mort Crane will let them." She gave a dismissive wave, as if consigning the Crane character to perdition. "Now, about this Lawson. I believe I had a wanted poster come through about him."

The sheriff said, "Yes, I remember the name. He killed a guard breaking out of prison. That's why there's such a big reward."

Adam looked from marshal to sheriff. "He also shot a friend of mine in order to steal a couple of horses. No need to kill him other than just plain meanness."

Aubrey slashed the air with his hand. "Like I said, doesn't leave witnesses. The man has to be stopped. But, why did you feel that was your job?"

"The man Lawson killed served with me in the Army. When we got out, all Lance wanted was to live peacefully on his small spread, marry, and start a family. I became a bounty hunter but planned to retire and set up in some little business. I'm ready to retire from the bounty game but I won't stop until my friend's killer is either dead or back in prison."

The sheriff pointed at Adam. "Listen now, we don't hold with killing a culprit unless he can't be captured alive."

Adam held out both hands. "Don't worry, I'm not one of those who'd shoot a man in the back to get a reward."

He noticed the spatula he held was dripping grease and returned it to the pan. "I won't shoot the scoundrel at all unless there's no other way to bring him to justice. I want Lawson back in prison where he has time to regret his ruthlessness before he's hanged."

Garnet sped in with a load of dirty dishes. "Joey, Hyacinth, time for you to go to school. You'll need a warm jacket this morning." She immediately loaded up more plates before she left.

Joey donned his jacket. Hyacinth tried slipping out without one.

Joey stepped between his sister and the door. "You're supposed to wear a coat."

The little girl gave a toss of her golden curls. "It smooshes my sleeves so they don't look as pretty."

Adam pointed his spatula at her. "Young lady, you heard your aunt say you should wear a jacket. Do as she said."

With a pout, Hyacinth stomped to the low row of pegs on which her coats and sweaters hung. "Oh, all right. I don't know why everyone always bosses me."

When the children had gone out the back door, Cordelia chuckled. "Those two are another reason Garnet needs help here."

Adam turned back to the skillets. "I agree even though they seem like nice kids."

Garnet brought in an empty coffee pot and collected a full one. "Adam, would you start another pot brewing? And I need three eggs over easy."

"Coming right up, Mrs. Chandler." Adam dumped the grounds into the large slop jar. A man collected the edible refuse for the Rafter O Ranch's swine. Soon Adam had more coffee on the way. He broke three eggs into the skillet but they turned crusty and brown around the edges.

Garnet was back and peered at the pan. Her face was flushed from hurrying and a few tendrils had escaped her hairdo. She was a beautiful woman who created yearnings he had no business having. He was tempted to lean forward so he could kiss her full, pink lips but that would be inappropriate. He'd better get his mind back on Lawson.

He met her gaze. "Sorry, I've ruined these."

Her blue eyes sparkled with humor. "Um, maybe I should do this order."

Adam stood aside. "Tactfully said, Mrs. Chandler. I'm better at scrambled eggs. I can cook meat, beans, and coffee on a campfire, but that's the extent of my culinary skill. Actually, I think eating is where I do my best work."

The sheriff laughed. "Just when I was admiring your prowess in the kitchen, Bennett. Guess you're not that different from me, after all."

Garnet adjusted the flue then slid the crusty eggs onto a plate she set aside. She chose three eggs and broke them into the same skillet. Flawlessly, she flipped the eggs and soon moved them to a fresh plate, added a slice of ham, a scoop of potatoes, and gathered a basket of biscuits covered with a napkin. With a smile, she backed against the swinging door and exited the kitchen.

Adam stood with hands on his hips. "She makes cooking appear so easy. I hope I don't ruin anything else. She's letting me sleep in the storeroom and eat in exchange for my help."

Cordelia clapped him on the back. He fought not to wince because she'd struck a sore spot. But, most places on his body were sore.

The marshal said, "Glad you're here to help her. We'll keep a look out for Lawson. He won't be far if he wants Garnet's jewelry. Might be something else he wants in this area."

Aubrey appeared to be deep in thought then he looked up. "We need to take that wanted poster and show it to all the businesses in Wildcat Ridge. If Lawson's here, he'll need grub and feed for his horses."

"One of which is my horse and two that belonged to Lance plus my mule. I want my animals back as well as the gear. That rat thought he took everything I had. My fall down the ravine kept him from getting a couple of things." He told them about Lawson's companions wanting his coat and boots.

The sheriff speared him with a gaze. "Let's hope Lawson doesn't learn you're here until you're recovered. We'll get on our way and see what we can learn. We'll keep you posted."

***

When Garnet and the children had gone to bed, Adam launched his plan to regain his strength. Lifting things for Garnet had worked out some of his kinks. She appeared delicate and frail, but she had to be strong to have managed the chores on her own.

With one hand he lifted a chair over his head three times then did the same with the other hand. He'd planned to repeat that on each side, but he had no stamina for more. Using a can of peaches for each hand, he sat on the chair. He raised the can from his arm outstretched to bent to his shoulder then straight up over his head.

Next, he did pushups. Every muscle in his battered body reminded him he needed rest. Tomorrow, he'd work more tomorrow. Now, he had to sleep.

Chapter Five

Garnet's nerves were taut as fence wire. Three nights with no prowler didn't reassure her. Frank Lawson wouldn't be so easily discouraged. She was waiting for him to strike again. How had he discovered where she'd gone?

She'd known him all her life, and been afraid of him that long. Even as a child he was a bully. His idea of a practical joke was mean-spirited. He was also vicious around animals.

Whenever possible, Garnet and her mother had avoided Frank. The problem was, Frank visited her great-grandmother often. Garnet loved her great-gran, who lived with Garnet's grandmother. There was simply no way to avoid seeing Frank if she wanted to see the two grandmothers.

Great-Gran had passed away during Frank's trial. Garnet had a forgiving nature, but that didn't apply to Frank Lawson. She was certain knowing he was a criminal had hastened Great-Gran's demise.

When they'd closed for the day, Garnet got ready for tomorrow's rush. "Thank you again for helping, Adam. You have no idea what a difference your presence has made."

In her mind, she thought of him as the bearded giant. He wasn't really much taller than Michael had been. He was broader in the shoulders and appeared more imposing.

"The least I can do in exchange for room and board. You need someone helping permanently, Mrs. Chandler. Once Lawson is captured and in jail, I'll have no excuse to remain."

"I know, and I have conflicting wishes. I want Frank captured and back in prison but I enjoy having your help."

She didn't add that she wished he would stay. How could she? Why would a man want to remain in the café's storeroom instead of moving on to something more permanent?

GARNET

As she was lining up supplies for the next day, someone rapped at the back door. She jumped as if shot.

"Want me to answer?" Joey asked.

She shook her head and motioned Adam into the storeroom. "No one's supposed to know Mr. Bennett's here, remember?"

When Adam was safely hidden, she opened the door to the alleyway. Tommy Bridges, son of the telegrapher, stood there.

"Hello, Tommy. A wire for me? Just a moment." She opened the cupboard and retrieved a nickel from the dish of loose change she kept for such occurrences.

When he'd gone, she tore open the telegram.

She dropped to sit on the stairs. "Oh, no!"

Adam hurried out of the storeroom. "What's happened?"

Joey and Hyacinth ran over to her.

Tears welled in her eyes and overflowed as she gathered the children to her. "It's from your grandparents." The telegram slipped from her fingers.

Adam bent to retrieve it. He read aloud:

Arriving Wednesday STOP Single woman not suitable guardian STOP. Taking children to live with us STOP

He held the paper. "You do a fine job with them. I know you love them and they feel the same for you."

Terror crossed Joey's face and he grabbed her arm. "Don't let them, Garnet. Please don't let them take us."

Hyacinth clung to Garnet's neck, sobbing. "I don't want to go with them. Grandpa and Grandma are mean."

Adam raised his brows and his eyes held question. "When did you last see your grandparents?"

Joey clung to Garnet. "When our great-grandmother was dying we went there. We hated it."

Garnet hugged each child to her again. "Dessie talked about her parents. They're far too . . . um, I don't know how to put it."

Joey raised his head and tears streaked his face. "Like sister said, they're just plain mean. Mama didn't even want to go visit them but she wanted to say bye to her grandmother."

Adam glanced from her to Joey. How long ago was this? Maybe they're nicer now."

"I was seven and now I'm eight. I bet they haven't changed. They were mean to Mama when she was growing up and mean to Papa when he wanted to marry her. They were mean to us when we were there. They say children should be seen but not heard."

Garnet's stomach churned and knotted. One week to get ready for the Millers. "They confuse being narrow-minded with being Christian. When she was growing up, Dessie had to sit on the sofa all Sunday afternoon while wearing her best dress. Her older brothers had to sit there while wearing their church clothes. Her parents thought it would be sinful to play on the day of rest."

He shook his head. "Inconsiderate, but hardly cruel."

"That's just one example. They believed in 'spare the rod and spoil the child'. Dessie had scars to prove it. She told me many times that if anything happened to her, she wanted me to raise the children."

Adam tugged on his beard. "I see. Did she put this in writing?"

Garnet shook her head. "Only a handwritten copy but nothing witnessed."

She pulled both children to her again. "Oh, what am I going to do? I don't want to think about not having these precious children with me. Or about them growing up in unloving circumstances."

Adam thought for a second. "Is there a lawyer in town?"

Garnet brightened. "Yes, Owen Vaile."

"You still have time to see him this evening. More than you will in the morning."

"You're correct. Children, you stay here and behave for Adam while I go talk to the lawyer." She kissed each one. "I intend to fight to keep you."

Adam picked up Hyacinth and laid a hand on Joey's shoulder. "What say we go to the table and play a game? You two choose."

Garnet drew on her coat and hurried toward the lawyer's. In her rush down the street, she bumped into someone.

GARNET

"Whoa, Garnet. What's the hurry?"

She looked up to find she'd run into Mayor Hester Fugit, who was with the lawyer Garnet needed to see. "I'm sorry, Hester. I'm so worried it's a wonder I didn't walk into the side of a building."

Garnet nodded to the mayor's companion. "As a matter of fact, I was hurrying to find Mr. Vaile."

He gave a slight bow without dislodging Hester's hand from where it rested on his arm. "Here I am, at your service."

Hester's smile lighted her face. "Why don't we go to my place so you'll have some privacy but can confer in comfort?"

"Oh, thank you, Hester. The most horrid thing has happened but I'll wait until we're in your home to explain."

The three walked quickly to Hester's house only a couple of blocks away. When they were in her parlor, Hester hung her coat on a hall tree.

"You two have a seat. I'll prepare coffee while you two talk." She walked into the kitchen portion of downstairs.

Garnet explained her dilemma. "Is the handwritten designation good enough?" She held her breath while she waited for his answer.

"Since she didn't have it witnessed or notarized, I'm afraid it isn't quite sufficient."

Garnet's heart sank to her knees. "Dessie's parents are so harsh. She had no joy in her life until she married Joe. You should know the children want to stay with me."

Owen leaned back in his chair and drummed his fingers on the chair arms. "Frankly, the court would favor the children's grandparents since you aren't even a blood relation."

Garnet leaped to her feet and paced the small room. "You must understand that I *have* to find a way to keep these children. In addition to the fact it's what their mother wanted and what they want, I can't bear to be parted from them."

Owen's expression held sympathy. "Is there a chance you could marry right away? That's the only instance I can see of you keeping them."

Hester carried in a tray loaded with what they'd need to have coffee. "Is there a single man in the area who attracts you?"

Garnet reclaimed her seat on the couch. "Well… there's one possibility." She looked into Owen's eyes. "You're sure that's the only way?"

"I am. You'd be taking a big chance with a trail."

"There's a bounty hunter who's been helping me at the café. He was beaten and robbed." She set her cup back on the saucer and explained about the prowler and why she'd asked Adam to stay.

Owen smiled and rubbed his hands together. "Sounds like a possibility. You could wed in name only and the children's grandparents would never know the difference."

He held up a hand. "Understand you'd be risking your café, though. You know if you're married your husband has a controlling interest."

Hand her café's control over to a stranger? Not likely. "That wouldn't do. He'd have to sign an agreement that he wouldn't claim any of my property. Would that work?"

Owen grinned and winked at her. "If I prepare the document, you can be sure it'll stand up in any court."

Hester poured the coffee. "Do you think this man would agree to a marriage of convenience?"

"I don't know. I guess I'd better ask him. If he won't, I'll find someone who will. Go ahead and prepare that agreement."

Hester smiled at each of them. "Glad that's settled—or almost. This is exciting. So much is happening."

Garnet did a double take. If she didn't know better, she'd think the mayor was blushing. Hmm, perhaps she and Owen were serious about one another. Wouldn't that be lovely?

GARNET

Chapter Six

As soon as Garnet could do so politely, she thanked Hester and Owen and hurried home. She found Adam and the children at the kitchen table involved in a card game.

Before she thought, she snapped, "Gambling? You have the children playing cards now? Good heavens, Dessie's parents would condemn me on that alone."

Adam glanced up from the cards he held. "Those people aren't here, we're not gambling, and this game teaches the kids to count."

Both her niece and nephew gaped at her.

She sat at the table, fighting to calm herself. "I apologize for being rude. I've . . . I've let that telegram upset me too much."

Adam stared at Joey, who pondered a moment before laying down his cards. "I win."

With a smile, Adam gathered the cards then looked at her. "What did you learn from the lawyer?"

"Just a moment." She turned to her nephew. "Joey, would you put your sister to bed tonight? Don't forget your prayers."

"Aw, okay." The boy took Hyacinth's hand. "We'll be praying Grandpa and Grandma don't take us with them."

She gave each child a hug and kiss. "Don't worry, I have a plan to keep you both here with me. I need to talk to Adam but I'll check on you when I come up in a little while."

When she was certain the children were upstairs, she lowered her voice. "I need to talk to you about a . . . a complicated possibility that would involve your help."

Adam raised his eyebrows. "Sounds intriguing. You have my full attention."

"The lawyer pointed out that I'm not a blood relative like Dessie's parents are. He thinks the only chance I have of keeping custody is if I'm married."

Adam watched her with a shuttered expression.

She took a deep breath. Drat, she'd hoped he would volunteer. "Since you're here anyway, we could enter a paper marriage and then you could get an annulment once the Millers had gone back to Wyoming."

He leaned back in the chair, both hands gripping the table's edge so tightly his knuckles were white. "Just like that, huh?"

She held up a hand to stay a protest. "Look, I know it's a lot to ask. You understand how much the children mean to me and that they prefer to remain here. Their mother chose me, even if she didn't get to finish the process. I'm sure it would only be for a little while and then you could go wherever you wish."

"And what if I didn't wish to go?" His voice was terse. "Have you considered that? What if I decided to stay her and continue the marriage?"

The idea left her dumbfounded. "Oh."

Shaking her head, she waved that incredible question aside. "Well, I don't think that's likely. Our life is usually pretty dull considering what you're used to." She shrugged a shoulder. "But, you could remain in Wildcat Ridge if you wished."

She didn't care whether he went or stayed but certainly there would be an annulment. Surviving the Millers' visit was why she needed his cooperation. "In any case, I'd need you to sign a document renouncing any claim on the café."

A dangerous smile appeared. She couldn't say why she thought it was both a smile and dangerous. Maybe because of the fire that snapped in his dark blue eyes and threatened peril. He must be a formidable person to cross and she'd insulted the bearded giant.

She leaned over and touched his arm. "Adam, please believe I meant no offense. I love these children. As tiring as running the place is alone, I even like the café. You must understand why I feel obligated to protect my livelihood and care for the children."

She withdrew her hand, conscious of the warmth of his skin beneath the shirt. "I know you're in the business of capturing wanted men and that you'd be losing money by taking out time for my plan. You'd have time to heal plus room and board, though. Um, I-I don't really have much cash to spare, but I can give you a garnet brooch and bracelet."

He'd leaned forward slightly but still sat staring at her.

She heaved a sigh. "Adam? Would you please say something?"

He eased back in the chair but his expression remained inscrutable. "So, just to recap, you want me to play your husband but without the marital rights. Then, when you dismiss me, I'd just ride off as if we'd never met. Is that right?" His voice carried a sting.

"You make me sound . . . um, cold and unfeeling. Surely you know very well I'm thinking of the children. Neither has recovered from losing their parents. In addition to being uprooted they'd have a horrible life with their Miller grandparents."

She stretched out her hands toward him. "While their material needs might be met, they'd receive no nurturing or expressions of love." She hated that her voice sounded whining and pleading.

Trying for a more professional tone, she said, "You'd have the jewelry to sell when you got to a city."

"How do you plan to convince the Millers that we're a couple? Aren't they likely to spend their visit living here with you?"

She brushed a hand across her forehead, wishing she could as easily whisk away the pounding inside her head. "I haven't thought ahead that far. Their wire sent me into a panic."

Hope seeping into her heart, she looked at him. "Does your question mean you're at least considering my proposal?"

"I'm considering *all* the facts." He leaned forward and tapped the table. "Have you forgotten about Lawson?"

"Since you told me he's out of prison I can't stop thinking about him. As if he isn't enough trouble, now I have the Millers to deal with."

"Lawson isn't going to leave you alone, you know, not until he's captured or dead."

"Do you think I don't know that? As long as I can remember, he terrorized me whenever I saw him."

"How am I going to keep my presence a secret if I'm married to you and parading around town? Have you forgotten I intend to bring Lawson and his two buddies to justice and collect the reward? That reward is my stake for my future." He tapped the table with each question.

She assessed his appearance. He'd need new clothes and a haircut. Most of all, he needed a trip to the bath house. "Has Frank seen you without a beard?"

His eyes narrowed and his right hand stroked his whiskers. "Hey, I like this beard. Have it shaped just the way I want it."

"I like it, too, but beards can grow back. You didn't answer my question."

Adam crossed his arms on his broad chest. "No, Lawson hasn't seen me clean shaven."

"If you shaved off the beard, he wouldn't recognize you, would he? I'll furnish you new clothes from the mercantile."

He slapped the table with both hands. "I can see how this is going." He muttered a curse word under his breath. "I might as well give in and agree with your plan."

Garnet leaped up. She caught herself before she hugged him. "Oh, thank you, thank you, thank you. You're doing a wonderful thing, Adam."

With an air of defeat, Adam conceded, "Guess I owe you this much. You rescued me when I was weak and badly injured. Must have been a scary sight when I came to your door."

He held up his hand. "But, I reserve the right to have my say in what goes on here. I'm not willing to be a puppet with you pulling the strings."

Oh, dear, what sort of *say* would he want? Her life was getting more and more complicated. But, then so was Adam's.

"I don't expect you to be a puppet. Having you here has helped me a great deal. Knowing you were down here at night gave me peace of mind so I could sleep. I can't explain why, but I feel this arrangement will work."

GARNET

Chapter Seven

Lying on the storeroom cot later, Adam couldn't believe he'd agreed to Garnet's crazy plan. Her pleading had torn at his insides. In the few days he'd been here he'd developed admiration for her and fondness for the children.

He understood her panic at the thought of losing Joey and Hyacinth. The prospect would be worse so soon after losing her husband, his kin, and countless friends. And, in Adam's opinion, the children didn't need to be distressed by removing them from their home. They obviously adored Garnet.

In spite of that, he couldn't forget about Lawson and his friends. By now, there might be more than two with the killer. Adam still hadn't discovered why Lawson had come here. Was stealing Garnet's gems the only motive?

He should have told her he didn't intend to accept her brooch and bracelet. No, let her think she was hiring him. Better that way than her knowing he couldn't resist the entreaty in her deep blue eyes.

When she came downstairs the next morning, she stopped short. "Y-You shaved."

He rubbed his fingers over his jaw. Felt strange. "Guess your husband shaved down here. Found a razor on the shelf under a small mirror in the storeroom."

"Because of the hot water in the range reservoirs, he found shaving in the storeroom easier than upstairs." She tilted her head and assessed him. "You look very different."

"I hope so. I'd hate to have lost my beard for nothing."

"I'm going to the store for your clothes as soon as the breakfast crowd is over. You'll need to tell me your sizes and what style clothing you prefer."

"Style?" He shrugged. "Pick out what you want. This is your show."

She blinked, appearing wounded by his remark. This was why he was still single at twenty-eight. He never knew what to say around a woman.

"Mrs. Chandler . . . Garnet, I trust you to pick out what's appropriate."

She took a deep breath and tied her apron strings. "Thank you, Adam. Now I'd better get breakfast for the children."

"Have you thought what you're going to tell them? Whatever you say has to sound convincing when repeated to their grandparents."

Her answer was interrupted by the two children clomping down the stairs.

Joey reached the kitchen first. "Adam, you shaved your beard. You sure look different."

"You think I'll pass this way?"

"Sure but you look like a different person."

He scooped up Hyacinth. "What do you think, Princess Hyacinth?"

She put a hand on each side of his face. "Now you're not a bear."

"Why did you think I was a bear?" He growled and tickled her stomach.

She giggled. "When you first came, you looked like a bear."

He set her in her chair at the table. "I guess I did, with all that mud on me. Remember, that's a secret and you can't tell anyone how I came here."

She crossed her heart. "We remember. If someone asks, we just say it's comp... complicated and they should ask you or Garnet. What will you tell people?"

"Don't worry about that, dear." Garnet set a bowl of oatmeal at each place. "Eat your breakfast. No school today so you can help Adam and me or play games inside."

"Maybe Tessa will come play with us."

"That would be nice, wouldn't it? If I see her mother I'll tell her to send over Tessa. Perhaps some of the McNair children might come, too. We'll see."

GARNET

Adam quickly finished his breakfast and resumed helping Garnet prepare for customers. He was amazed she had as much business as she did. Most town residents were struggling to make ends meet.

Her prices were low and the food exceptional. In addition, there was the social aspect of seeing neighbors and chatting. Business included the stage drivers and passengers as well. He predicted the café would always be profitable.

***

During the slight lull between breakfast and lunch, Garnet made a quick trip to Tweedie's store. She chose three changes of clothing, a new coat, and new boots. George Tweedie frowned when he totaled her purchases and added them to her bill, but didn't question her. He was too busy with other customers today.

When she returned to the café, she removed the hand-lettered sign announcing *"Back in a few minutes"* and unlocked the door. A bell overhead would let her know when a customer entered so she went into the kitchen.

Adam unpacked her purchases. "I have boots, why did you get another pair?"

"You said one of the men who robbed you wanted yours. They're quite distinctive so I figured if he saw them, they would give away your identity."

Admiration was in his expression. "Good thinking. I've caught men with only that much of a clue. Glad you aren't taking up being a bounty hunter."

She smiled at him, pleased he appreciated her effort. "Do you have another occupation I can use when I introduce you to people? Announcing you as a bounty hunter would be sure to get to Frank."

"I have a ranch in Colorado. My brother owns the adjoining spread and is managing mine for me."

"That sounds nice and respectable. Eunice and Harold Miller should find that suitable. Joey, Hyacinth, did you understand what Adam said? He has a ranch in Colorado."

Joey looked up. "You have horses and cows?"

Adam nodded. "I do, but my brother takes care of them for me and we split the profits if there are any."

Hyacinth came to tug on Adam's sleeve. "Would you get me a pony?"

He chuckled. "Sorry, Princess Hyacinth, I don't happen to have one handy."

Further conversation was prevented by the lunch customers. Adam's help made so much difference. She dreaded thinking of the time he'd leave. Perhaps by then she could hire someone part-time.

What would she do if the Millers insisted on staying with her? She and Adam would have to share the same bedroom. My goodness, how would that work?

She could sleep on a pallet on the floor and he could have the bed. Except, he was gentlemanly and probably would insist he sleep on the floor. She was borrowing trouble. When the time came, they'd work out that solution.

When they were finished for the day, she joined Adam and the children in a game of cards. She was proud of Joey and Hyacinth for being able to count and match the cards so well. Later, after she'd put the children to bed with a chapter from *Aunt Louisa's Oft Told Tales*, she returned to the kitchen.

GARNET

Chapter Eight

Adam looked up from the kitchen table, where he sat reading the volume of *Tom Sawyer* she'd loaned him. "Ah, good, I hoped you'd come back down so we could talk."

"Yes, we need to discuss arrangements and get our stories straight." She sat across from him. "I dislike lying, but I see no way around it."

"Stick to the truth as much as possible. Now, tell me about yourself. What brought you and your husband here?"

"He came with his first wife and they set up this café with money inherited from her family. She and her baby died in childbirth."

She took a deep breath and met his gaze. "I came as a mail-order bride from Georgia. When my parents died they left only debts. By the time those were paid, I had no money and nowhere to go. I was living with my grandmother when I answered Mike's request from a matchmaker. He asked for a wife who was a good cook and would help him with the café."

Adam was incredulous that such a beautiful woman didn't have a long line of beaus. "I'm surprised you didn't have numerous suitors."

"You must not be from the South. Most of the good men died in the war or went West. The second crop is younger than me, but many of them left too. Frank is an example of those single men left in our village."

He didn't want to even contemplate her with a man like Lawson. "In that case, I'm not surprised you chose to leave. How long had you been married?"

"Only nine months. At least I had enough time to learn how to run the café. I don't mean to sound unfeeling. Mike tried to be a good husband, but he wasn't very practical. I gather his first wife was even more fanciful. That's why we have glass chandeliers in the dining room and such nice dishes."

His picture of her husband wasn't very flattering. "Very contradictory to mining town clientele and I did wonder. Tell me about growing up."

"I had a lovely early childhood. We lived in a small town near Savannah. My parents were loving and kind. Before the war, Papa's family had been quite wealthy. Before I was born, of course. He still dreamed of rebuilding his fortune."

She sighed at the memories. "Unfortunately, all he acquired after he'd paid the carpetbaggers' fees were debts."

Adam had heard about the stiff taxes levied on Southerners. "I grew up in Colorado near Telluride. Cold in winter but there's good grass there. Still, don't know whether or not if I'll go back."

"But, isn't it family land? I'd think you wanted to hold on to it because of that."

He couldn't explain how complicated his decision was. "My brother—his name is Benjamin—wants to buy my share. He inherited the homestead so my part doesn't have a house on it. When I'm there I stay with him and his wife, Angela."

"Do they have children?"

He smiled recalling his brother's children. "Joey and Hyacinth remind me of my niece and nephew named Bennie and Beth. They're about the same age and there's also little Bart who's four. Beth looks like Angela with dark hair and brown eyes. Bennie and Bart look like my brother."

He tugged at his cuffs. Garnet had laundered his muddy things but he alternated them with those she'd bought him. "That reminds me that I need a bath in the worst way. I've tried washing but it's not the same. Is there a bath house here?"

"Daryl Comer operates a bath house and barber shop. He's open on Sundays if you'd like to go in the morning."

"I take it you don't attend church."

"Usually we do but I'll miss tomorrow to get ready for our uninvited visitors and our wedding. Sunday is the only day I close the café."

"Is your minister going to come calling if you aren't in church tomorrow?"

A cloud crossed her expression. "Our minister was one of those who died. A positively evil man named Mortimer Crane owns most of the town. He plans to dismantle the church and move it to one of his other sites. He's already moved some of the other buildings."

What kind of man would tear down a church? "How do you propose getting married if there's no preacher in town?"

"People wire the minister at the next town. He rides over and performs the wedding, then rides back." She laid a hand at her throat. "Oh, the lawyer I talked to is a Judge. Perhaps he can perform the ceremony."

"Would you handle that?"

"I'll do so while you're at the bath house. The children can go with me."

"Garnet, we have to come up with a plausible story for how I arrived and why I'm here. I can say I came here because I was looking for horses. That's the truth in that I'm looking for my horses."

She nodded and smiled. "We met when you came for a meal. That's also true. Oh, but how did we get together and get engaged?"

"I noticed you're a gorgeous woman and that you had no one to help. As a way to get to know you I offered my services."

"Why would you do that?" She waved away his suggestion, obviously not understanding how attractive she was. "Maybe your horse threw you and you were injured. No, think of something."

"My brother is supposed to meet me here but he's delayed. I had time to kill so I decided to use it to get to know a pretty woman better. When I learned you had a prowler, I was insistent I protect you and the children."

"That might work. The prowler was Sunday night, and you came on Monday. Cordelia will likely go along with our story."

She rose and came around the table to lean over him and peer at his face. "The cuts are about healed and the bruises are fading. By Tuesday, they won't be noticeable."

"Okay, we're getting married on Tuesday. I'll let the man at the bath house know in case he gossips."

"I don't think he does, but the owner of the mercantile does, trust me. He'll be wondering why I bought men's clothing. Saturday is when the farmers and ranchers come to town and he was too busy to ask questions. He'll grill me next time he sees me."

"Tell him you didn't like the clothes I brought. Not acceptable for a mining town."

She chuckled. "That's certainly true. They weren't acceptable for anywhere, not in the condition they were in when you arrived."

She laid a hand at her throat, a gesture she seemed to use a lot. "I feel so much calmer. Thank you for agreeing to marry me. I'll go up and get ready for bed. I'll be able to sleep now that we've worked out a plan."

He picked up the book he'd been reading and watched her go upstairs. They hadn't worked out everything. Sleeping arrangements held a special interest for him.

GARNET

Chapter Nine

Garnet sent Adam to the bath house as soon as she thought it would be open. He wore his new boots and yesterday's clothes and carried a fresh set of duds to wear after he'd bathed.

She and the children enjoyed a leisurely breakfast before going for a walk. She headed for Hester's as it was still too early for church services. "You two play quietly on the porch or front yard. I won't be long."

As she suspected, she found Owen there having breakfast. "Just the man I wanted to see. Can you perform marriages?"

He leaned back in his chair and sent her a wide smile. "I can and have. I take it that fellow is going to cooperate."

"Fortunately for me, he is. We thought Tuesday at eight might be a good time to wed. Will that be satisfactory?"

"It will unless Hester has another obligation."

Hester beamed at Owen. "Tuesday evening is a fine time." She turned back to Garnet. "When are these grandparents arriving?"

"On Wednesday's stage. They'll be in a bad mood, I'm sure, after that bumpy ride. From what Dessie said, they aren't very likable people in the first place. What I don't know is if they're staying at the Ridge Hotel or if they plan to stay with me."

"Let's hope they choose the hotel." Hester shook her head. "From what you've said, though, they'll stay with you. I'll bet they're as frugal with their money as they are with their affection."

A cloud of dread encompassed Garnet. "Oh, you're probably right. I guess I'd better make arrangements for them. They can use Joey's room and he can sleep on the couch."

Hester sent her a knowing look. "Keep them as far from your bedroom as you can."

Garnet felt the heat of a blush spread across her face. "I intend to. I hope they won't go poking into things, but I imagine Mrs. Miller will. From what Dessie said, her mother has no sense of privacy."

Owen dabbed his mouth with a napkin. "Where do you intend the ceremony to be held?"

"In the café dining room." She explained the story they were giving of Adam's arrival and courtship designed to appease the Millers. She didn't elaborate on the real reason Adam was in town.

Hester glowed with happiness. "All the weddings are so hopeful, don't you think?"

Garnet was pleased her friend was coming out of the deep depression she'd been in from losing her husband and son. Of course Hester would never stop loving them or forget them, but at least she was able to smile now and to keep company with Owen Vaile.

Garnet grinned at the lawyer. "Yes, and the newcomers who've decided to remain give me hope, too."

In usual lawyer style, he gave nothing away in his facial expression.

With the arrangements settled, she bid Hester and Owen good day and gathered her niece and nephew. On their way back to the café, they met Eleanora and Tessa.

After greeting them, Garnet asked, "Can Tessa come spend the day with us?"

Tessa tugged her mother's skirt. "Please."

Her mother patted the girl's head. "Sounds like a nice day to me. Don't let her be a bother now."

"No, she never is. By the way, you and Tessa and Reed are invited to my wedding on Tuesday." She gave the details and mentioned Eleanora could spread the word if she wished.

"Will you be at church today?"

"Not today. I have so much to do in preparation for the wedding and the children's grandparents' visit. You can announce the wedding for me, though."

Next, they went to the marshal's office. Cordelia wasn't there so they crossed the street to her house. Briefly, Garnet explained her

GARNET

plan. Cordelia agreed to support that explanation and said she'd tell the sheriff when he came for dinner.

With three children in tow, she went back to the café. When she saw Adam, she stopped dead in her tracks.

"You're blond." She couldn't help staring. His hair was the color of wheat in summer when sunshine turns it golden.

He brushed his hand over his hair. "Once again, thanks to the bath house and some Scandinavian ancestors. Man, that hot water felt good. Comer trimmed my hair a bit, too."

Garnet couldn't get over how handsome Adam was. She'd known he was attractive, but cleaned up, he left her awestruck.

He picked up Hyacinth. "What do you think, Princess Hyacinth?" He tickled her tummy.

She rubbed a hand on his face. "I like how you look."

He set her down and laid his hand on Joey's shoulder. "What about you, Joey?"

Her nephew tilted his head and peered up at Adam. "I liked you before but you look, um, real good now."

Adam gestured to Tessa. "And who is this lovely young lady?"

Hyacinth took Tessa by the hand. "This is Tessa. She's our friend. She comes here sometimes when her mom is busy. We like for her to be here."

"Glad to meet you, Tessa."

Hyacinth tugged Tessa's hand. "Come on, let's go play upstairs."

The three sounded like several times that many children going up the stairs.

Watching their progress, Adam grinned. "Be nice to have that much energy, wouldn't it?"

He faced her. "Wedding set?"

"Yes, the lawyer is also a judge and is going to perform the ceremony on Tuesday at eight in the dining room. Is that all right?"

He shrugged a shoulder. "I left that up to you so that's fine."

"If you follow me, I'll give you a tour of the family rooms. When I arrived, I was surprised they're as comfortable as they are."

"I'd like to see them." He followed her up to the parlor.

"The furniture was all expensive, as you can tell." She shook her head. "Not at all practical for a café owner in a mining town, but I enjoy it so I don't mind that they splurged."

She gestured to the side. "There's a tiny kitchen but we seldom use it. Joey's bedroom is here. I tried to make it look like a little boy's room."

She'd painted the pink papered walls light blue. The dark blue coverlet appliquéd with white sailboats made it more masculine. She'd bartered meals with the undertaker to build book shelves for Joey's toys and his few books. She'd figured correctly that if Alex Terry could build a coffin then he could build other things as well. She'd painted the shelves white.

Adam put his hand at her waist. "Looks like a room any boy would love."

She hated to pull away from him, but she moved down the hall. "Next is Hyacinth's." The pink striped wallpaper was perfect for a little girl. Her niece had white shelves, too. The three children sat on the floor on a rug made by Dessie.

Joey looked up, appearing slightly miffed. "We're playing house and I have to be the father. Later we're going to play sheriff and robbers and I get to be the sheriff."

Garnet smiled at him. "Thank you for taking turns, children." She was nervous about the next room. There was no avoiding it, though, so she took a deep breath and gestured. "Here's the master bedroom."

Adam stood inside the room and gazed around. He leaned his hands on the mattress. "Appears comfortable. Nice room." He picked up the broken drawer. "I can probably repair this for you."

"I'd love it if you can. That dresser is a quality piece of furniture and I hate that it's ruined."

He wandered down the hall, peering at each picture and shelf. "I'll see if there's glue on hand. If not, I'll get some from the mercantile."

He grinned at her. "That will give the owner a chance to meet me so he can gossip about me."

GARNET

She opened the hall linen closet. "I'll get you a spare set of sheets for the cot? I'm sure you'd like clean ones since you're clean."

He accepted the fresh bedding. "I appreciate you thinking of that."

"I'd better go make some dinner."

Adam patted his stomach. "I could eat and I'll bet the kids can too. I'll change the sheets while you whip up a meal."

He stepped in front of her at the stairs. "I had strict instructions from my mother. Men go behind a lady going up the stairs and in front of her coming down so they can catch her if she falls."

"Sounds nice in theory, doesn't it, but I fear we'd both fall in such a circumstance."

After lunch, Garnet suggested the children rest for an hour. She knew Hyacinth and Tessa would fall asleep. Adam helped her in the kitchen and then picked up the book she'd loaned him.

"Would you like to read in the parlor? The chairs are more comfortable."

"This is fine until after Tuesday. I might take a nap myself."

"Sundays are the days for napping and reading. Also for mending and such."

"And I'll bet for laundry. You did my laundry during the week. Is that typical?"

"That was an emergency. Actually, there's a woman in town who does laundry and I prefer to send ours to her. She really needs the business and she doesn't charge much."

"You support one another here. That's nice."

Memories flared and she couldn't prevent the veil that enclosed her. "We lost so many—not just relatives but close friends. We had to work together or give up. A few did give up and went back to their original homes or moved on to another place. Those of us who stayed are the more determined not to be defeated."

Three-year-old Tessa came down stairs rubbing her eyes. "I was sleepin' but Hyacinth kicked-ed me."

Garnet picked her up. "I'm sorry, sweetie."

Adam gestured to the storeroom. "Put her on the cot."

"Are you sure?" When he nodded, Garnet carried the little girl to the storeroom. "Look, this is like your own room while you're visiting us. Here's a special bed just for you with fresh sheets on it."

"Goody. No one will kick me here." Tessa smiled when Garnet tucked the cover under her chin and kissed her.

"Sweet dreams. When you wake up you can play some more."

Garnet went back into the kitchen. Now she was stuck downstairs. She decided to catch up on her mending.

GARNET

Chapter Ten

By the next day, news of the wedding had spread through Wildcat Ridge. If the circumstances were different, Garnet would be as elated as she pretended for her friends. She contemplated her plight as she went through her usual chores.

She'd married one man she didn't know and things hadn't turned out too badly. Mike was a nice man and she'd become fond of him. If she were honest, she had to admit she hadn't grown to love him and doubted she ever would have. He was too immature.

Although she grieved for all those who died in the explosions, most of her grieving had been for Dessie rather than for Mike. Dessie had become like a true sister to her in the few months they'd worked together. She missed all her friends who'd died, but she missed Dessie most of all.

Heavens, here she was, about to marry another stranger. Sure, Adam appeared to be a nice man. Would he keep his word? At times the way he looked at her made her nervous. Like now.

Adam appeared with arms laden. "I'm moving my belongings to the bedroom. Plenty of time but I want to be sure I get every trace of me out of the storeroom."

"Leave the cot for next time Tessa spends the day. I emptied a couple of drawers in the chest for you and there's space in the armoire for you to hang clothes." Having his things in her bedroom created an odd sensation in Garnet. She chided herself with a reminder that she was lucky Adam had agreed to this charade.

He passed her as he climbed the stairs. "Thanks. Found some wood glue. I'll mend that cracked drawer today while I'm thinking about it."

"Great. I've hated that lovely dresser was damaged. Just like Frank to thoughtlessly destroy something nice."

Adam paused and leaned over the railing. "The marshal hasn't seen anyone matching his description. I feel like he's still here. Don't think he'll leave without your jewelry."

"I don't either. It's a priority with him. He's too close to miss out on snatching the gems. He's probably hanging out in one of the bad saloons. There's one that I don't think even Cordelia dares go in to check."

"You can bet that would be the one he'd choose." He continued toward the bedroom.

Their bedroom.

Dear merciful heavens, what a dilemma.

He was handsome as sin and polite. He'd told her he wasn't very nice, but that's not what she'd seen. He was helpful to her and good with the children.

Was there another side to him yet to become evident? There must be for him to capture criminals. She hoped he could hold his own against Frank but keep the nice side for her and the children.

***

Garnet was so nervous she was certain she could jump out of her skin. She wore her best dress, not that it was fancy. The gown was a watercolor print of lavender cotton. Her light brown hair was in tight curls on top of her head with two long curls falling down her shoulder.

"Be still, Hyacinth. You want to look your best for the wedding, don't you?"

The little girl momentarily stopped squirming. "I didn't know old people like you and Adam got married. He said he'll be my uncle now. Is that right?"

"He sure will. We'll be your old, old aunt and uncle." She affixed a large pink bow in the girl's blond curls.

Hyacinth twirled around. "Is Tessa coming?"

"I'm not sure, dear. We'll see in a few minutes. Don't muss your dress and hair. I'm going to check on Joey."

Joey appeared in the doorway. "I'm ready. Adam helped me."

Adam followed Joey. "We men have to stick together, right, Joey?"

Joey beamed with happiness. "That's right."

GARNET

Garnet took a deep breath. Joey admired Adam so much. What would happen when Adam moved on? She couldn't solve that problem now. Her wedding was in a few minutes. One thing at a time.

"I guess we should go to the dining room. Guests will arrive soon."

Adam grinned at her. "You'll be surprised. Your friends have been busy." He gently held her arm. "Don't hurry or you'll fall. Won't be a wedding then."

When they entered the dining room, several of her friends were there. Earlier Adam had stacked the tables at the back and set chairs in rows. Someone had moved two of the tables together with a lovely white cloth covering them.

A large wedding cake set on one table. On the other side was a punchbowl filled with what appeared to be apple cider. Cups and plates from the kitchen were stacked on the two tables along with forks.

Garnet clasped her hands together. "This is wonderful."

Rosemary hugged Garnet's shoulders. "The cake is from the Sugar and Spice Bakery. Cordelia donated the apple cider. The punch bowl belonged to Blessing's mom."

Thalia stood behind the table. She sent Dinky Moon a stern look. "My job is to make sure no one dumps liquor into the bowl."

He held up both hands. "I'm cured, my love. I wouldn't even consider doing something like that."

Everyone laughed. When his first wife left him, Dinky had become a sad alcoholic until Thalia had taken him in hand. Now he was back operating his newspaper, the *Wildcat Ridge Journal*.

Thalia sent Dinky a loving glance. "I know that, dear."

Owen Vaile arrived with Hester on his arm. He wore his customary suit with a waistcoat that coordinated. Hester was dressed as usual in a loose dress. This one was soft pink and enhanced the glow of happiness on her face.

Garnet smiled at the friends who'd come to prepare for the celebration. "I can't tell you how much this means to me. You're so kind and thoughtful. I almost tried creating a wedding cake but there just wasn't time. I'm glad now."

Off to one side Owen and Adam examined papers. Her groom didn't look happy. After he glanced at her, he signed where Owen indicated. Good, her café was safely hers into the future.

Hester shepherded Garnet and Adam to the appropriate spots as Owen took his place facing them. Garnet heard the creak of chairs and shuffle of feet as people took their seats. Calm enveloped her—the marriage seemed very real.

Joey and Hyacinth sat on the front row. Hyacinth swung her feet with a smile on her face. Joey was solemn and acted far too grown up for a boy of eight. With Adam's help, perhaps Joey would learn to be his age and play.

She couldn't help feeling optimistic. Her lovely friends had made certain her wedding would be special. Adam had been congenial and cooperative. Today was a special day, no matter the reason behind the wedding.

Owen cleared his throat. He appeared dignified and austere but she had learned he had a soft heart and a fun sense of humor. Proving her opinion, his eyes twinkled as he met her gaze.

"Friends, we are gathered here today to celebrate the marriage between this couple." His additional remarks were brief before he led into the actual vows.

"Garnet, do you take this man to be your lawfully wedded husband, to love, honor, and cherish him, rich or poor, in sickness and in health, forsaking all others and cleaving only to him?"

Garnet didn't like lies or pretense. She had trouble reconciling her situation with the marriage vows. Taking a deep breath, she said, "I do."

"Adam, do you take this woman as your lawfully wedded wife, to love, honor, and cherish her, rich or poor, in sickness and in health, forsaking all others and cleaving only to her?"

Adam looked into her eyes and smiled. "I do."

From that look alone, Garnet thought she would melt at his feet. His smile warmed her through and through, touching places she believed were frozen.

Owen looked at Adam. "Do you have a ring?"

GARNET

Acting embarrassed, he fished in his pocket and pulled out her own ring she'd given him. She knew using the ring Mike had provided bothered Adam, but buying a new one was an unnecessary expense.

Owen grinned. "You may kiss the bride."

Adam swept her into his arms and kissed her as if he loved and adored her. He must have practiced kissing a lot because he was excellent at it. Her knees went weak and heat shot through her.

Applause and catcalls rose behind them. When Adam broke the kiss, he appeared as happy as any groom. She appreciated him acting his part.

Hyacinth tugged on his jacket. "Are we married now?"

He picked her up and pulled Joey beside him. "We are. Now I'm officially your uncle." He looked into Garnet's eyes. "We're a family."

Garnet insisted she would take care of cleaning up but her friends paid no heed. The women washed the dishes and the men restored the tables and chairs to their correct places.

Rosemary said, "You go on up to your rooms. When everything is spotless as you keep it, we'll lock the doors behind us."

Garnet was humbled by her friends care. "Thank you, each of you, for a wonderful wedding."

Once they were upstairs, she looked at Adam. "Do you feel as awkward as I do?"

He grinned. "Probably not. Let's get the children to bed. I'll tuck in Joey."

Insides quivering, Garnet managed to get Hyacinth to bed, heard her prayers, read her a story, and kissed her goodnight. She heard Adam and Joey talking when she went to her bedroom. Only it wasn't just hers now.

Quickly, she donned her nightgown and robe then hung her dress in the armoire. Seeing Adam's shirts hanging beside her dresses reminded her she'd taken a big step. Would he abide by her wishes?

Chapter Eleven

Garnet lay with the cover up to her chin. She couldn't suppress troubling memories of her first night here as Mike's bride. She'd been terrified and he'd rushed through consummating their marriage.

She'd cried in spite of trying not to. Since she hadn't really known what to expect, to say she didn't enjoy the experience was an understatement. The next time, he was gentler and she lost some of her fear. From talking to Dessie, however, Garnet knew her and Mike's marriage was not like it was supposed to be.

Mike was a little boy in a man's body, always putting his needs and desires first. His big brother, Joe, had looked out for him all his life and Mike took it for granted. Perhaps Mike had done his best.

The one time he tried to look after Joe had led to Mike's death. Sadly, Dessie and many of their friends also died. Guilt and grief washed over her. Why was she the one to live?

No, she was through crying. This was her life. She had her café and was taking steps to insure she kept Hyacinth and Joey with her. Deep, slow breaths helped calm her.

Adam was smiling as he came in and closed the door softly behind him. "That Joey is a smart young man. He figured out this marriage was so you could keep him and Hyacinth here."

She knew her eyes widened and she sat up. She opened her mouth to answer him.

Adam held up his hand. "Joey promised not to tell anyone. He won't forget. He's more mature than a lot of adults I've met."

"I know he is. I hope without the threat of his grandparents he can be more a little boy. He's such a good child."

Adam unbuttoned his shirt. "He worries about you and his sister. I told him I would take on that job and he could concentrate on school and play. Made him happy and he settled down with a smile on his face."

She forced herself to look away while he peeled off his clothes. "Thank goodness. Oh, but what will he think when you leave?"

Her new husband sat on the bed to remove his boots. "Don't worry about it. Remember, I've taken on the job of worrying. Leave it to me while you concentrate on running the café and raising these children."

"I enjoy both of those things."

"I'll help all I can but I also have to capture Lawson. You won't be safe until he's either dead or back in prison."

A shudder went through her at the mention of her cousin's name. "I'd thought I was safe from him when he went to prison. That didn't stop him last time."

Adam crawled under the cover. "Do you know how he learned your whereabouts?"

She lay perfectly still on the edge of the mattress. "If he was in contact with any of the family, including his father, the word probably got around about where I'd gone."

Adam pulled her closer. "I'm not going to attack you so get off the edge or you'll roll off."

"I-I didn't want you to think I was a tease."

He lay with his hands beneath his head. "I doubt you've ever intentionally teased a man. However, all you have to do is look at him or swish by and that works."

"You mean you?" She was surprised to learn she'd attracted his attention in that way. She'd tried to act professionally.

"No point denying it. Now, go to sleep before I forget my promise. Those grandparents arrive tomorrow. Should be an . . . um, interesting day."

Interesting as in the Chinese curse, *May you live in interesting times.* "Goodnight, Adam, and thank you."

"No more thanking me. Goodnight, Mrs. Bennett." With those words, he rolled over and faced the other way then went to sleep.

***

Adam had feigned sleep last night so Garnet would relax. She worried about everything and not without reason. He'd lain awake thinking about what he'd created for himself. A wife, two kids, and a killer required his full attention. How was he going to stretch himself to accomplish what he needed to do?

This morning he woke and pulled on his clothes. Garnet roused when he got out of bed.

He shoved his feet into his boots. "I'll go start the coffee while you dress."

"I'll be right there." She looked inviting pushing her hair away from her face and a sleepy look in her amazing blue eyes.

Adam figured that was his cue to leave the room. He headed for the stairs, stopping to stick his head in Hyacinth's room. "Time to get up, Princess."

The little girl mumbled, "I'll bet real princesses get to sleep as late as they want."

"When school's out you can sleep later. Today is when your grandparents arrive. Have to look sharp."

"I don't want to see them. I wish they'd stay where they live and leave us alone."

"They're arriving this afternoon and there's nothing we can do but greet them." He stopped at Joey's room. "The start of a new day."

"I bet you're surprised I'm already dressed." Joey's hair stood up like a cockscomb.

"I know you're a sharp boy. Soon as you comb your hair, come on downstairs."

The boy clapped a hand on his head. "Aw, I forgot my hair."

Behind him, Garnet said, "You sure did. I'm proud of you for already being dressed."

Adam descended the stairs ahead of his wife. She was right on his heels.

He stoked the range embers and added coal. "What are you planning when the stage arrives? Are you closing the café?"

She set the coffee pot on the range top. "Why should I? They know where we'll be. They can find us."

"Have they been here before?"

GARNET

"Once, about a year after Dessie and Joe moved here. They didn't approve of the town then. I'm sure they'll like it even less now."

Rubbing his hands together, he grinned. "Doesn't matter. We're ready for them."

He turned her toward him. "When they get here, don't jump if I touch you. We have to appear in love, and that means I need to touch you and you need to do the same for me."

She appeared to mull over his suggestion. "I suppose you're right. Even though according to Dessie they're not demonstrative, they'll expect newlyweds to be. They'll also expect me to know your birthday and how old you are."

"Good thinking. I was twenty-eight on June 20. How about you?"

"On August 16, I was twenty-one."

"You grew up in Georgia, right? And I grew up in Colorado. Would you give me a call when they arrive?"

That afternoon, Garnet rushed into the kitchen. "The stage just rolled in. Adam, I'm so nervous."

He moved a pan off the range. "I'll come out with you."

The driver and the shotgun rider hurried to claim a seat. They only had half an hour's stop and were always hungry and in a hurry. Several people stepped from the stage. All but two headed for the hotel.

She peered out the window. "That couple must be the Millers. Don't they look solemn? Maybe they're just tired."

"I'll bring the stage men their meal." Adam disappeared into the kitchen.

Garnet couldn't stop watching the couple.

The man was tall and thin and slightly stooped. His graying hair was just long enough to show under his bowler hat. He carried two suitcases. The woman with him was chubby, dressed in black, and wore a disapproving expression.

When the couple was inside the café, the man set the suitcases by the door.

Garnet walked over to them. "I'm Garnet, are you the Millers?"

"We are." The woman answered, her brown eyes narrowed. "You're not wearing mourning."

"So many died at once, Mrs. Miller. Those of us left have had to proceed as well as we can. Most don't wear black due to finances."

Adam appeared and set plates heaped with food in front of the stage driver and his shotgun rider. He quickly came to Garnet's side and placed a hand at her waist.

She looked up at him and smiled. "Mr. and Mrs. Miller, this is my husband, Adam Bennett. Adam, meet Eunice and Harold Miller, the children's grandparents."

Eunice Miller stiffened even more, if possible. "You've already remarried? Have you no sense of decency?"

The few diners still present viewed them as if they were on a theater stage.

Before she could stick up for herself, Adam came to her defense. "My wife is the most honorable and decent of women. You are in a town that had an unimaginable tragedy. The residents had to move on quickly to survive. Don't judge them by other standards."

Garnet bit her tongue to keep from telling this woman where she could go. Thank goodness Adam had spoken before she'd said something rude. "Will you be checking into the Ridge Hotel or did you plan to stay with us?"

Harold Miller fiddled with the brim of the hat he held in front of him. "No need for the extra expense of a hotel when we can stay here with the children."

Garnet gestured toward the kitchen. "Let me show you to your room. The stairs are in the kitchen."

Adam poured the stage's men more coffee.

She heard Cyrus Carson, the driver, say, "Go on and take care of family business. If anyone else comes in, I'll give a holler."

Adam joined her and the Millers as they trekked upstairs. "I'll take one of those cases for you."

Harold Miller said, "I'll let you. You look up to the task."

Garnet showed them where they'd stay. "I don't know where you stayed before but you'll sleep here in Joey's room. If you'll give me a few moments, I'll have fresh sheets on the bed for you."

GARNET

Eunice's face looked as if she'd swallowed something bitter. "You mean the children don't share? Look at this fancy room, you're spoiling them. It's a good thing we've come to get them."

Garnet faced them, ready to give these people the sharp side of her tongue. Standing behind them, Adam shook his head slowly. In the few seconds it took for his action to register, she regained control.

"Why don't you have a seat in the parlor? Adam, would you show them where that is in case they've forgotten?"

He sent her a smile. "Right this way, folks. You'll find ours is a comfortable place."

Cyrus hollered, "You've got customers."

Garnet abandoned the sheets and rushed to the café. Certainly her business came before those awful people.

Adam came back to the kitchen. "I gave them the sheets and told them you need my help."

"Thank you, I do, especially for controlling my temper." She dished up bowls of stew.

He put biscuits in a basket and covered them with a napkin for her. "We can get into the custody situation when the café closes."

Garnet watched for the children after school. Since they were aware this was the day their grandparents arrived she hoped they wouldn't dawdle.

Joey and Hyacinth came into the café walking as if going to the guillotine.

Garnet leaned over them to speak privately. "Your grandparents are upstairs. Remember, be polite. No matter what they say, *you are staying here* with me. Do you understand?"

Joey looked at Hyacinth then back at her. "You promise?"

Could she? "I give you my promise I will do everything in my power to keep both of you here with me. But, these are still your grandparents and must be treated with respect."

Hyacinth scrunched her face as if about to cry. "Do I hafta see them? Couldn't you go with us?"

"You know I have to serve our customers. Now, go say hello to Adam and then go upstairs and see your grandparents."

Her heart ached for the children. They were so afraid. So was she. What if Owen was wrong and she couldn't keep Joey and Hyacinth? Then, her heart would break

GARNET

Chapter Twelve

Garnet turned the sign to *Closed* with relief. Since the Millers had arrived, she had been curious about how things were progressing upstairs. When she entered the kitchen, she found both children at the table. The Millers sat with them instead of waiting in the parlor.

Joey had a pencil and a sheet of the brown wrapping paper she saved for the children. "Grandpa, I hafta practice my spelling words."

Hyacinth held her doll. "Molly likes to watch me write my name and letters."

Garnet started setting up for the following day. She discovered Adam had almost finished washing up and had set out some of the things she'd need.

She leaned into him. "Thank you."

He hugged her shoulders and planted a kiss on her temple. "Hold fast. I'll help all I can."

When they were through in the kitchen, she walked over to see the results of the children's homework.

"Very good, Joey. Hyacinth, your little G and Q need more practice so they don't look the same. Remember the curly tail is different for each." She demonstrated for her. "You're getting so much better, though. I'm proud of you both." She kissed each child on the head.

She served supper with Adam's assistance. They had ham, green beans she'd canned last summer, potatoes, carrots, and apple pie. The children drank milk and the adults had coffee. After they'd finished, she and Adam tidied the kitchen while the Millers visited with the children.

She finished and turned to her guests. "After the children do their school work and we eat, we usually play a game. Perhaps you'd be more comfortable if instead we went upstairs to the parlor this evening."

Eunice shook her head. "No, we want to see just how the children have been spending their time."

Joey looked at Adam. "Can we play cards?"

Garnet froze. A poor choice.

Adam put his hand at her waist. "If Garnet approves."

"Of course." She sat beside her niece. "The children have been learning to match numbers and shapes and count using cards in a simple game."

Clearly from their facial expressions, Eunice and Harold were outraged, but they were silent. Garnet figured they were logging instances to prove her unfit. Well, she had to be honest about how she was raising Joey and Hyacinth.

Adam shuffled the deck. "You'll join us, won't you, Harold, Eunice?"

Harold frowned and crossed his arms. "We don't hold with playing cards, young man. We'll watch."

Adam dealt. The game lasted far longer than it would have with all adults playing.

Joey laid down his last card. "I win."

Hyacinth put down her cards. "I like checkers more because I win sometimes."

Joey smiled at his sister. "Okay, next time we can play checkers."

Hyacinth clapped and spoke to the doll she'd left on the table. "Yay, did you hear that Molly?"

Garnet pushed the cards toward Adam. She lighted another lamp and handed it to Joey. "Time for bed, children. I'll be up in just a moment to tuck you in and read a story."

Joey hopped up and then carried the lamp carefully. "Will we finish *Robinson Crusoe*?"

"We'll see. Don't forget to wash your face and hands." She turned to her unwanted guests. "Shall we all go up?"

Eunice struggled to her feet. "I am awfully tired. I won't mind turning in early."

"Joey will sleep on the couch. Hyacinth is a kicker and he wouldn't get much sleep sharing with her."

GARNET

Eunice appeared surprised. "Oh, Dessie was a kicker, too. I couldn't keep her covered."

"Hyacinth stays covered but kicks under the cover. After the disaster, she slept with me sometimes. I'm sure I had bruises."

"What about Joey?"

Garnet chuckled. "He asked me to sleep in the middle so she wouldn't kick him. I didn't mind. We were all so lost it was comforting to be together."

Eunice grew misty-eyed. "I still can't believe our baby is gone. Life just isn't fair."

Garnet couldn't help feeling sympathy for the woman even though she didn't like her. Losing a child would be horrific. "No, it isn't but we're doing the best we can to recover."

She thought she should change the subject. "You saw where the bathing room is. Do you need anything else?"

Adam said, "I put a pitcher of water and a glass in your room in case you're thirsty during the night or have medicine to take." To Garnet, he said, "I'll make up Joey's bed while you hear their prayers and read to them."

Later in hers and Adam's room, Garnet crawled into bed and heaved a huge sigh of relief. "So far, I haven't lost my temper and yelled at the grandparents. You've been so much help, Adam. I don't know what I would have done without you."

"You don't need to wonder because I'm here and at your service." He gave a deep bow before lowering the lamp and then stripping before he joined her.

Without anyone knocking, the door opened and Eunice stuck her head in. Light from the lantern she held spilled through the open doorway and highlighted Adam's bare chest.

She gasped. "Oh, I beg your pardon."

Adam sat up. "May I help you, Eunice?"

"I was looking for the bathing room but I must have gotten turned around."

Joey called, "I'll show you, Grandma."

She backed up and closed the door.

Adam whispered, "You buy that?"

"She's been here too long to get lost. Obviously, she was checking to see if we're sharing a bed."

"And, we are. She doesn't need to know more than that."

Joey's voice carried from the parlor next door. "Grandma, you should never open the bedroom door of married people. Mama said you knock and wait to be invited inside. They might be having a private husband and wife discussion."

Eunice snapped, "I said I got turned around."

Garnet clapped her hands over her mouth to stifle her giggles. Beside her Adam shook with silent laughter.

When they'd composed themselves, Adam said, "What a great boy."

GARNET

Chapter Thirteen

The next day, Thursday, time crawled for Garnet. She wondered what Eunice and Harold were up to but was too busy to keep tabs on them. Not that she had anything to hide—at least not something they could discover—she simply didn't like snoops.

That evening, Harold looked at Joey and Hyacinth. "We'll be taking the children home with us on the Saturday stage."

Garnet stiffened. Hyacinth started crying so Garnet pulled her niece into her lap.

Joey appeared frightened. "We want to stay here, Grandpa. We want to live with Garnet and Adam."

Garnet looked from Eunice to Harold. "The children *will* remain here with me. Dessie chose me to look after them in the event of her death. Your objection was that I'm single, but you can see I'm now married."

Eunice sniffed. "Barely, and you should still be in mourning. I'll bet you only married to try and keep the children."

Adam stared at Eunice. "For your information, Eunice, the minute I saw Garnet I knew she was the one for me. You can see how attractive she is. Even better is that she's kind and compassionate and caring. How could I not ask her to marry me?"

"Then, who sleeps on the little bed in the storeroom?"

Joey stood. "That's where Tessa sleeps."

Eunice frowned. "Who is Tessa?"

Hyacinth clapped her hands. "She's my friend even though she's little. She has to take naps."

Garnet smoothed hair from the little girl's face. "Eleanora is one of the widows who's just remarried and Tessa is her daughter. I look after the child at times, especially before her mother remarried. She's a sweet little girl."

Harold slapped a hand on the table. "That has nothing to do with this situation. Dessie was our daughter and we intend to raise her children."

Garnet set her niece on the girl's feet. "Joey, you and Hyacinth go upstairs and play while I speak with your grandparents."

Sobbing, Hyacinth clung to Garnet. "Don't make me go with them. I wanta stay with you."

Garnet whispered to her niece, "Remember what I told you earlier, you and Joey are staying here with me." Aloud, she said, "Go upstairs with Joey."

Her nephew took a still sniffling Hyacinth by the hand. His eyes were sad when he looked over his shoulder at the adults. "Come on, sister. We can play in your room."

Her poor children were so frightened. So was she. She prayed hard that she could keep the children. Probably Eunice and Harold prayed they could.

When the children had climbed the stairs, Garnet turned to Eunice and Harold. "Dessie left me written instructions to raise Joey and Hyacinth. She also made me verbally promise several times that if anything happened to her then I would raise her children."

Eunice looked askance. "Why, that's ridiculous. You only knew her a few months. We're blood kin."

"Dessie and I bonded instantly and were like sisters. She spoke often of growing up and said that was not how she wanted her children raised."

Eunice shook her head. "I find that hard to believe. She's not here to speak for herself so you could say anything."

Harold pointed at her. "If you have written permission from our daughter, let's see it."

Garnet rose and opened a drawer and took out a sheet of paper. "This is a copy I made before I gave our lawyer the original."

Eunice snatched it from her hand and she and Harold put their heads together to read what amounted to a will.

To Whom It May Concern:

GARNET

I, Dessie Chandler, am the mother of Josiah Chandler, Jr. and Hyacinth Chandler. If I die before they're grown, I want Garnet Chandler to raise my children. She understands how I want them brought up and the values I find important. The children already love her and she loves them.
Signed by my hand,
Dessie Miller Chandler   January 15, 1884

Eunice laid the paper on the table. "I don't believe she wrote this. You're making it up to steal our grandchildren."

Garnet's heart pounded. "You can speak to the lawyer tomorrow."

Harold harrumphed. "Some crooked backwoods lawyer won't make a bit of difference to my opinion."

"He's not just a lawyer. He's also a Judge of the Supreme Court of Utah Territory. His name is Cornelius Owen Vaile but he doesn't use Cornelius."

Both Millers appeared as if cold water had been thrown on them. Eunice opened her mouth but spoke no words.

Harold didn't give up easily. "You better believe we'll speak to him. Where's his office?"

"He's using the mayor's office for now. I'll show you in the morning, but I won't be able to go with you."

Harold sent her a belligerent glare. "We'd just as soon go on our own. Don't need you prompting the lawyer."

Adam spread his hands. "Look, I know losing your daughter was terrible and something no parent should ever have to face. Garnet still grieves for her as if they really were sisters. But, think about the children. They've lost their parents, their uncle, plus friends. Garnet is their one link to security. Moving them now would only deliver another blow."

Harold crossed his arms. "Maybe so but they'll get over it. They need to be with kin."

Eunice stood. "This is so upsetting. I need to lie down, Harold. Let's go up to bed."

For Garnet, the next few days felt as if she walked barefoot on glass shards. Adam helped immensely but she sensed him growing restless. That escalated her anxiety.

What would she do if he left to chase Frank? How could she explain that to the Millers? What if Frank returned to the café?

After talking with Owen, the Millers postponed their departure. When they'd been there a week, she couldn't stand the strain any longer. That night after they'd gone to bed, she shared her fear.

"Adam, I know you're eager to capture Frank. Please, don't leave while the Millers are here."

He turned and laid his arm over her, nestling his face in her hair. "I intend to catch Lawson but don't want you to worry. Cordelia and Aubrey believe they spotted him coming out of the mercantile but he rode off before they could follow him."

"I hope he doesn't come back to the café."

"Remember, whatever happens, I'm not running out on you. Now relax, surely the Millers will leave soon."

With his arm across her, she drifted into sleep.

GARNET

Chapter Fourteen

Several days later at noon, Garnet was surprised to see Mortimer Crane and two of his cronies enter the Crystal Café. Saturday lunch was always busy. At least today Eunice was trying to help serve customers.

Joey and Hyacinth also helped. Harold sat in a corner and read a newspaper. Why couldn't he do that upstairs or in the kitchen and free up one of the dining room tables?

Eunice carried a coffee pot and went around refilling cups. Joey carried a pitcher of water for those who chose that to drink. Crane gestured wildly as he spoke in a loud voice with his friends.

Eunice barely stepped out of the way in time to prevent dousing the man with hot coffee. Joey wasn't so lucky. Crane knocked Joey's arm and sent the water pitcher into the man's lap.

Joey's eyes rounded and he picked up the pitcher. "Gosh, I'm sorry, Mr. Crane."

The two men with Crane reacted by shoveling in food as fast as they could.

Spewing curses at Joey, Crane leaped to his feet. "You careless brat, look at me, I'm drenched." He looked at Garnet. "Well, aren't you going to whip the boy?"

She advanced on the group and handed a towel to Crane. "You were swinging your arm around as you talked. It was as much your fault as anyone's."

From the kitchen, Adam heard the disturbance and strode into the dining room. "You can't use that kind of language in a family establishment."

Crane pointed at the boy. "That useless, idiotic brat poured water on me." He let loose another string of curses. "Boy deserves to have his rear blistered."

Joey was in tears. Hyacinth hid behind Garnet's skirts.

Adam put his hand on Joey's shoulder. "Joey is neither useless nor a brat. He's the finest young man you'll ever meet. This boy is worth at least ten of you and your kind."

Crane responded by cursing at Adam.

Adam stepped in front of Joey. "Get out, Crane. We don't need your business."

Crane was almost a foot shorter than Adam, but he puffed up like the dandy he was. "Do you know who I am? I'm Mortimer Crane and I own this town."

Adam leaned into the man's face. "You don't own this café. If you can't speak respectfully in front of women and children then you need to stick to your bordello and saloons. Leave now or I'll throw you out."

Crane gestured to his two companions to follow. "I'm leaving but you'll regret this."

One of the men stood but shoved a last bite in his mouth before following his boss and his coworker.

When they'd gone, Adam looked at the others in the room. "Folks, I apologize for the disturbance."

Those dining applauded him. Garnet beamed at him.

Harold put down the newspaper he'd been reading and stood. "I'll get the mop." He disappeared into the kitchen.

Joey wiped his eyes on his sleeve. "Thanks, Adam. Do you really think I'm a fine boy?"

"You better believe it. You're the best boy I've ever met. And Princess Hyacinth is the best girl. Aren't I lucky to know both of you?"

Joey hugged Adam. "I love you."

Adam was poleaxed by Joey's declaration. What should he say? His eyes met Garnet's tear-filled gaze.

He lifted the boy into his arms. "Why don't you help me in the kitchen for a while? I could sure use a good helper like you."

Hyacinth ran after them. "I'll help, too."

What was he going to do about his almost-family? These three had become too important to him. He dreaded his coming encounter. What if Lawson won again?

GARNET

Garnet and the children were only now beginning to work through their grief. Even though he'd been here a short while, he'd sunk roots. Roots that went far deeper than he would have believed possible in this length of time.

He had to make sure he came out ahead of Lawson this time.

After they were in bed that night, Garnet turned toward him. "Thank you so much for defending Joey. He'd decided you don't like him as much as you do Hyacinth because you call her princess but don't call him prince."

He leaned on his elbow. "You should have told me sooner. What did you tell him?"

"I said it's because he was older and didn't need to be coddled like a little girl."

"Poor little boy. I meant what I said. He's a fine young man. He'll be a responsible adult."

Garnet appeared to mull over something. "I told Joey and Hyacinth not to argue with their grandparents, that you and I will handle making sure they stay here."

"Apparently they've done as you requested. You should lecture me—I've had trouble not challenging the Millers myself."

She said, "Pffft, so have I. Many times I've almost told them to move to the Ridge Hotel next door. The only reason I haven't is I feel sorry for their having lost their only daughter. They have two sons who were several years older than Dessie, each of whom is married with children. Losing Dessie must be horrible for them."

In a few seconds, she braved a subject which had puzzled her. "Adam, I've wondered why you don't want to go back to your place in Colorado. Did you and your brother have a falling out?"

"Not exactly, but I doubt I'll ever live there. He and Angela kept trying to match me with her sister. Angela is nice enough even though I wouldn't enjoy being partnered with her. Her sister, though, is a shrew you couldn't pay me enough to marry."

"Not even garnets?"

He chuckled. "Not even her weight in diamonds. Every time I go there, they're at me to court her. The sister flirts and tries to get me in a compromising situation so I'll be obligated to marry her. I finally told her that no matter how she plots I won't marry her. I could visualize her making up something, though. So, I stay away."

"No wonder. Eventually, the sister will marry someone else and it'll be safe to go home." She was hopeful he would stay in Wildcat Ridge but she didn't tell him.

"That's not really where I think of as home any longer. I might as well tell Ben he can buy my half of the ranch. Are you shivering?"

She pulled the cover up to her chin. "I'm getting warm now. I wish we had a fireplace or stove in here. Hyacinth's room gets heat from the range below. Joey's is protected by the building next door. Since this one is on the building's corner, it's like an iceberg. Oh, well, I'm lucky to have the café and the living quarters up here. This room gets a nice breeze in summer. Goodnight, Adam."

"Goodnight, Mrs. Bennett."

Next to her, Adam congratulated himself on his control. Calling her by her married name was a deliberate attempt to remind her they were wed. He had wanted to suggest they could both get warm by snuggling. That would have been a bad idea as he would have been sure to get too friendly.

She seemed unaware of how attractive she was. Surely people had told her she was beautiful. If so, she hadn't taken it to heart.

He wondered about Garnet's first husband. Somehow, Adam doubted the man had given her the attention she deserved. Mostly, it seemed she was a work horse and bed companion. In spite of that, she retained an air of innocence as well as determination.

The marshal and sheriff had dropped by again. Lawson was rumored to be camped just outside of town, Adam figured likely in the tent that had been on his pack mule. No one had spotted the camp but one of the saloon patrons had tipped Cordelia that the man had been in with two others.

Aubrey rode out each day but hadn't encountered Lawson. Adam asked him not to go out alone looking for a backshooting killer. Aubrey said it was his job but agreed to wait a few more days.

Adam figured Lawson would make his move at the Harvest Festival coming up this weekend. Had the killer realized he was here yet? Would Lawson recognize him as he looked now?

GARNET

Chapter Fifteen

This evening, Garnet knitted in the parlor. She was making a sweater for Hyacinth in the pink the little girl loved. "This is the first year the town's had the Harvest Festival but it's sure to become an annual event. One last event before the heavy snow sets in."

Eunice was also knitting. "We'll be leaving as soon after the festival as the stage runs. We can't risk being trapped here all winter."

Harold's brow furrowed. "Our neighbor is watching our place until we get back, but he won't tolerate us being gone much longer. Don't much hold with festivals myself but Eunice wants to see this one. Always too much gambling and drinking and folks carousing."

Adam stuck a slip of paper in his book and closed the pages. "There'll be a lot of innocent activities. I hear there'll be a sack race, apple dunking, pie contest, and horseshoes."

At times like this Garnet wished he was her real husband instead of just on paper. "Don't forget the checkers tournament in the café."

Eunice knotted her thread and held up a red scarf. "This is for Joey so he won't feel bad when Hyacinth gets a sweater."

Garnet glanced up from her own knitting. "That's thoughtful of you, Eunice. I'm making him a red sweater next. He's growing so fast now."

Eunice actually smiled. "Teen years are when boys really grow. We had a hard time keeping the oldest one in clothes when our boys were that age."

Harold nodded. "Now they're getting a taste of that. Oldest grandson is sixteen." He sat straight and added, "Named Harold after me and his dad. Boy has a good head on his shoulders."

"You're fortunate your sons live near you." Adam laid his book on the side table. "If Joey wishes, he can take over the café, but he won't be pressured either way."

Harold reared back aghast. "But he's not your son. What if you have more children and one's a boy?"

Adam looked at Harold. "Joey is our son same as if he'd been born to us. And, Hyacinth is our daughter. We couldn't love them more."

"Well, I'll be dogged. Didn't figure on that happening."

Eunice pulled her handkerchief from her cuff and dabbed at her eyes. "We still haven't decided whether or not to go to court over custody. Hyacinth and Joey are all we have left of our darling Desdemona . . . Dessie."

Quickly changing the subject, Garnet said, "I forgot there will be a clothing exchange at the mercantile on Saturday. I won't get rid of anything for children in case Adam and I have children in the future, but many of the residents will be trading clothes."

Harold nodded. "Good idea. Save a lot of money that way."

Eunice laid her knitting supplies aside. "We should have thought of something like that when our children were young."

Garnet continued knitting on Hyacinth's sweater. "The situation here is desperate. So many of the town's residents are widows with children and no income or very small salaries. They simply haven't the funds to purchase necessities for their children."

Harold rubbed a hand across his chest. "The poor will always be among us. Can't help all of them. I believe I'll head to bed."

Eunice stood. "I'll come with you. Joey can't go to sleep until we get out of the parlor."

When they'd gone, Joey donned his pajamas. He'd sat in Adam's lap while Garnet read a story to him.

She ran her fingers through his hair. "Crawl in bed now."

He stood beside his temporary bed. "Grandpa doesn't care there are poor. Isn't that what he was saying?"

Garnet exchanged gazes with Adam. "I'm not sure exactly what he meant. Maybe he meant that so many people are poor he can't help all of them. We have to give him the benefit of the doubt because we don't know what was in his mind."

Joey crawled under the covers. "I still think he doesn't care about the poor."

GARNET

Garnet leaned over and kissed his forehead. "Goodnight. You're doing a wonderful job being respectful. I'm proud of you."

His smile rewarded her. "Goodnight."

Inside their room, Adam dallied with the clothes in his part of the chest. "Joey is a smart boy. He has Harold pegged all right. I'll bet the man has never given to the poor."

She knew he was giving her time to get into her nightgown and appreciated his effort. He was a gentleman in every way.

"From what Dessie said, you're right. I imagine they have quite a bit saved because she said they never spend a penny unless it's necessary."

"Makes me wonder if they use a bank or hide the cash in their home somewhere."

Garnet crawled in bed. "I can't see them trusting a bank or wanting the bookkeeper to know the amount of money they had. They're missing a lot of joy in their lives."

"They'd never have let a mud-covered stranger into their kitchen and fed him. I'm sure of that."

"Then they'd have missed getting to know a very nice person. I'm glad I know you."

"Thank you, Mrs. Bennett. I'm glad too."

She tucked the cover under her chin and closed her eyes. Here she was sleeping next to a man to whom she was married. Yet, even though they were wed, they'd had no intimate relations. In a way this had become normal to her. In another way, the situation was surreal.

Usually, she was optimistic and cheerful. Frank's prowling and the Millers' extended visit was changing her. The strain had her jumping at noises and expecting the worst. Without Adam's reassurance, what would she do?

Thank heavens, the Millers would only be here until Wednesday. Having them out from underfoot would help her and relieve the children. Poor dears were constantly afraid they'd be forced to leave with their grandparents.

What about Frank? He was a dangerous man at best, and he wasn't here on good behavior. There had to be a showdown between him and Adam, hopefully including Aubrey and Cordelia.

CAROLINE CLEMMONS

Dear Heavenly Father, hallowed be Thy name. Thank you, Lord, for sending Adam to help us. Bless him, Father, as his presence has blessed us. Protect Adam from harm. He's a good man. I ask that you keep Joey and Hyacinth in Your care also. I pray that they be allowed to remain with me. Bless all who live in Wildcat Ridge. Amen.

GARNET

Chapter Sixteen

Midmorning, Adam sat in the marshal's office. "Mark my words, Lawson will make his move during the Harvest Festival."

The sheriff pushed his hat back slightly. "I agree. Cordelia and I have deputized several men to help."

Cordelia held up a badge. "I can do the same for you."

He shook his head. "Thanks but I need the bounty and a deputy wouldn't be eligible."

Aubrey speared him with a stare. "The deputies will be spread out through town and will be watching for Lawson. What's your plan?"

"I see him striking at one of two places. One is the Wells Fargo safe. Second, and the one that scares me most, is Garnet and/or the children. Protecting them in a crowd will be near impossible."

Cordelia returned the badge to the desk drawer. "We'll do our best. I'm sure you will too."

Aubrey shook his head. "My suggestion is for you to stick close to Garnet all through the festival."

"I'll be like glue." Adam planned to be by her side the entire event. "In the meantime, all I have is a derringer that was in my boot when I was robbed. I'm hoping you'll loan me a spare revolver you took from someone. I give you my word I'm not trigger happy. I hope to capture that murdering scum Lawson alive."

The marshal opened a gun cabinet. "I don't approve of anyone but lawmen carrying firearms in town. In this instance, though, I think you'd better be prepared." She handed him a revolver, holster, and gun belt. "This belonged to a man who fought capture." From her desk, she handed over a box of ammunition.

After sticking the box in his pocket, he buckled on the belt and pulled his coat closed to conceal the firearm. He couldn't help wondering who had worn the gun before Cordelia acquired it. "I appreciate your trust and assistance. Now, I'd better get back and help Garnet in the kitchen."

Adam strode toward the café, wondering if Lawson was in one of the buildings he passed. If so, would the man recognize him? Adam rubbed his cheek. From what he saw in the mirror he appeared a different person. But, how would others see him?

He entered through the back door. Harold was prowling around the kitchen. Granted the man must be bored just hanging around while he and Garnet worked and the kids were in school. Would it kill him to lend a hand?

Adam hung his coat on one of the pegs by the door. "Anything unusual happen while I was gone?"

Harold closed one cupboard door and opened another. "Nothing except people coming into the café. I never realized so many people ate in cafés and restaurants. Where do they get the money?"

Adam had wondered the same thing.

Harold turned around and stared. "You're wearing a gun. What's that about?"

Drat, he'd forgotten Harold was here. "Town marshal deputized me for the weekend during the festival. Lot of strangers will be in town and she wants to keep things peaceful."

"Seems peaceful now." He closed the cabinet door and sat at the table. "Surprised Garnet can stretch to run this café even with your help. Looks run off her feet to me."

"Garnet's business will slow down soon. We mentioned the stage stops running after the first big snow, which will probably happen around the end of next week. Whole town changes. No school, no tourists, just residents."

Harold harrumphed. "Don't know what attracts tourists in the first place. Nothing unusual to see."

Adam pretended a graciousness he didn't feel. "There is. Next time you come perhaps we can go up to see Angel Springs. There are hot springs and people come to bathe in the waters for their arthritis and such. Heard it's mighty pretty up there with lots of flowers blooming near the steam that won't grow elsewhere on the mountain."

GARNET

Harold pulled at his ear lobe. "Reckon that would be helpful. Don't imagine we'll ever get back this way. We're better off at home."

Adam didn't express his opinion that they should have stayed in Wyoming in the first place. He lugged a large soup kettle half full of water to the range. While the water heated, he peeled potatoes, onions, and carrots.

Garnet came into the kitchen carrying dirty dishes. "Oh, good, you've started stew. Are there enough of those beef scraps left?"

"I'm ahead of you, my dear." He gestured to a bowl filled with bite-sized chunks of beef. "There are plenty for a hearty stew. Need more cornbread and biscuits, though."

He stood with arms outstretched to show off his weapon. "Marshal Wentz deputized me for the festival. Lot of strangers in town and she's deputized several men to help keep watch."

Her expression assured him she received the message. "There are a lot of strangers coming into town."

She looked at the kitchen clock. "Closer to lunchtime, I'll make the breads. Have you seasoned the vegetables?"

"Thought you'd want to do that." He leaned down and kissed her cheek, speaking low, "Don't worry. You keep your Colt in your pocket."

"I will." She laid a hand on his arm. "You're correct, kind sir. I'd also like to add a couple of jars of the canned tomatoes from the storeroom shelves." She quickly measured out salt, pepper, and a couple of spices.

He guided her to a chair. "You sit while you can. I'll get whatever else you want in the kettle."

Garnet sank onto a chair. "Royal treatment today." She looked at Harold. "How have you kept yourself entertained this morning?"

"Went for a walk through the town. Lot of excitement about this Harvest Festival. Kind of silly, if you ask me."

Adam hadn't asked him. He set the jars on the counter and opened them. "Things like the Harvest Festival help the town quite a bit. Create community. People here are close-knit." He poured the tomatoes into the stew and stirred.

The bell on the outside dining room door let them know a customer had come in. Garnet sprang to her feet and hurried to investigate.

Harold stared at the swinging door through which she'd just gone. "Girl doesn't let moss grow on her feet, does she?"

"She works hard and people respect and admire her. She still finds plenty of time for Hyacinth and Joey."

Harold sent him a triumphant look. "She still isn't blood kin. No way she can change that." He headed for the stairs. "Believe I'll go rest a bit. Won't have the chance once we get home."

Adam frowned into the stew. Good riddance to the man. Nosy old goat.

GARNET

Chapter Seventeen

Garnet tied a pink bow on Hyacinth's second braid. "You look lovely and your hair will stay out of your face. Let's see if the others are ready to leave."

Eunice approached them. "I still can't believe you're closing the café with so many potential customers in town."

"I'm only closing early. The checkers tournament starts at two, which is in a few minutes. I can't serve food with that going on. Joey and Hyacinth want to see the games."

Harold ambled toward them. "You certainly spoil the children. Eunice and I worry about them believing the world will pamper them."

She tried to keep her voice light even though she would like to rail against these two. The horrid way they'd treated Dessie was what they'd intended for Hyacinth and Joey. She couldn't allow that to happen.

"They already know firsthand that life can be difficult. All children—and adults, too—need to know their home is a place where they're special. I intend to make sure Hyacinth and Joey know how much they're loved and valued."

When they were outside, Eunice sniffed. "I might as well have stayed upstairs. I don't want to play any of these silly games."

"Perhaps you could go to Tweedie's Mercantile and help hand out clothes. Adam took Mike's and Joe's over for me yesterday. They need help and mothers will want to see their children in the games."

"I suppose I could do that if they have a chair so I don't have to stand too long."

Adam said, "They already had a couple of chairs and a table set up when I was there. You wouldn't have to stand."

Harold held his arm for Eunice to latch onto as they walked. "I know where it is and I'll see you there. Once you see how they're set up you can decide whether or not you want anything to do with them."

The Millers walked toward the mercantile but Garnet and her family stayed in front of the café. The games area was on Front Street in front of the Ridge Hotel and Crystal Café.

Adam laid his hand on Joey's shoulder. "Well, son, what do you intend to enter?"

"The ring toss and the sack race."

Hyacinth clapped her hands. "Me, too. I don't like dunking for apples 'cause you have to get your face wet."

Garnet took her by the hand. "The sack race starts a little later. Let's get you two in line for the ring toss."

They laughed together while watching the antics of other contestants.

Adam nudged the two. "Go ahead, children. It's your turn."

Joey accepted his rings. He placed one foot at the line and one behind then did a lunge forward. His ring landed on the peg. He did that two more times.

"I did it, I won."

He accepted a blue ribbon from Alec Terry.

Hyacinth stepped up. She tried imitating Joey and fell.

Garnet helped her stand. "Just throw the ring your way, dear. Don't try to be like Joey."

Hyacinth threw and missed each time. She started crying. "I wanted to win. I wanted a ribbon like Joey's."

Adam lifted her to his arms. "Not everyone can win, Princess Hyacinth. Remember, Joey is older and more mature."

Joey smiled. "Maybe you can do the sack race."

Children lined up with their legs in burlap sacks. Joey raced over to get ready.

Hyacinth shook her head. "Those look scratchy and dirty. I'll just watch brother."

Garnet noticed that when he lifted and carried Hyacinth, Adam's coat parted and glimpses of his gun and holster showed. She stood next to him, heart pounding and her own revolver in her pocket. He held Hyacinth with his left arm and had his right around Garnet. How would he get to the gun in time if assaulted?

She glanced at every stranger who passed them. Harold ambled to stand with them.

Adam turned to Harold. "We're waiting for Joey in the sack race."

Harold looked at the line of children. "Older boys than him are lined up, too, so I don't reckon Joey stands a chance."

"We're proud of him for trying. He won a blue ribbon in the ring toss."

She heard the annoyance in her husband's voice even though he was polite. Funny that after knowing him such a short time, she already knew the inflections of his voice and posture. He really was a remarkable man.

Hyacinth clapped her hands. "Go, Joey."

Garnet and Adam yelled encouragement, too. She was shocked when Harold let loose a big yell.

"Come on, Joey. You can do it."

Adam sent her a surprised smile which she returned.

The course was littered with children who'd fallen over. No one was hurt—many got up and kept going, others quit. Garnet laughed at the mayhem and Adam joined in. She even heard chuckles from Harold.

When the race was finished, Bert McNair won. Joey was fourth place.

He dragged his feet coming over to them. "I didn't win and didn't get a ribbon."

Adam ruffled his hair. "We're real proud of you. You held your own again larger and older boys and girls."

Joey looked up at him. "You're not disappointed in me?"

Adam knelt in front of him. "Of course not. You did your best and that's all anyone expects from you. We're proud of you for trying."

Garnet hugged his shoulders. "That's right. We're proud of both of you. Now, what shall we do next?"

Harold surprised her. "I believe I'll try my hand at horseshoes. I've been watching and it doesn't seem too hard."

"Joey and I'll go with you, Harold. What do you say, Joey, you want to try pitching horseshoes?"

"Sure."

Hyacinth tugged on Garnet's skirt. "Do girls play horseshoes?"

"I don't know. Let's go see." Garnet had held her niece's hand as soon as Adam set her down.

"Sorry, Hyacinth, there are no women or girls playing. Let's just watch Adam and Joey and Grandpa."

While they were there, Eunice wandered to stand with them. She was ashen.

Garnet touched Eunice's shoulder. "Are you all right? Do you need to sit down somewhere?"

Eunice took a handkerchief from her sleeve cuff and dabbed her eyes. "I never realized how poor some of the people here are. Yet, they're all so cheerful."

"We're sort of like a large extended family. We take care of one another when we can, offer comforting words when needed. You see, we survived a horrible tragedy by banding together and that's how we've gone on each day."

Eunice pulled her collar up around her throat. "Do you think Dessie was happy in this barren place?"

"I'm positive she was and she didn't think of it as a barren place. She and Joe were a truly devoted couple. They loved the children and showed they did every day. I've carefully followed Dessie's schedule for Hyacinth and Joey. Even though they lost their parents, they haven't had to endure other significant changes." She hoped Eunice got that hint.

Hyacinth hugged Garnet's skirts. "I love you. You always take good care of us."

"I love you, too, Princess Hyacinth. I'll always do my very best for you." She gestured to the horseshoe court. "Look, Grandpa and Adam and Joey are having their turn."

Hyacinth craned her neck this way and that. "I can't see."

Garnet lifted her niece. "Now you can."

GARNET

She felt Eunice's eyes watching her but she didn't care. If the woman didn't approve of showing affection in public then so be it. She wanted the children to always know they were loved.

Chapter Eighteen

Garnet saw Harold blush when he learned Eunice had witnessed his game. "Didn't hurt anything to pitch a few horseshoes."

Eunice sniffed. "Did I say anything to the contrary?"

He pulled at his earlobe. "No, but I know that face."

Garnet indicated the hotel behind them. "I hear they're judging the pie contest now. After they've finished, they'll cut the pies and sell slices. Shall we go inside?"

Adam peered over those in front of them. "The place is jam-packed. Eunice, why don't you wriggle in and find a seat. We'll wait out here until there aren't so many people."

"You wouldn't mind?"

"Of course not. Or, if you prefer, you can go to the rooms over the café and watch the goings on up and down the street."

Eunice brightened. "What a good idea. I'll go upstairs and look out the bedroom window. I'll see you later."

Harold nodded to them and rushed after his wife. "Wait, I'll come with you."

Adam leaned near Garnet's ear. "Finally rid of them and on our own. Are you enjoying the afternoon?"

"Watching the races with my family was wonderful. I hope this is an annual event."

"Sure to be." He gestured in an arc. "Look around us. People appear to be enjoying themselves. More people are arriving the later it gets. I hope you plan on dancing with me tonight."

"I didn't know if we'd go to the dance. I'm sure Eunice and Harold won't approve."

"Aw, they don't approve of much. Try to give yourself a break and forget about the Millers for a while."

GARNET

"Adam, I confess I can't completely relax. I examine every stranger's face. I wonder if he's one of Frank's gang. I don't know how you do this as an occupation. I'd go mad."

He scanned the crowd. "I've looked at everyone who's passed us. Believe me, this is my final case. After Lawson is captured, I'm retiring to a nice, normal job with no travel."

She hoped he'd stay in Wildcat Ridge. "The reward bounty should help you start whatever business you wish. Have you given thought to what that might be?"

"I've given it a lot of thought, Mrs. Bennett. When I have the cash in hand, then I'll share my decision with you. For now, things are too iffy."

"Man of mystery."

Joey tugged at Adam's sleeve. "Can we go sign up for the three-legged race? Hyacinth and I practiced at home."

Adam knelt to look the two in the face. "Are you sure?"

Hyacinth put her hand on his cheek. "I can do it, Adam. Brother helped me learn."

Joey laid his hand on Adam's shoulder. "We did it in the hall at home."

Adam stood and looked at Garnet with widened eyes, as if to ask what he should do.

She knelt in front of them. "The road won't be smooth like the hall. Remember how many children fell in the sack race?"

Joey clasped his hands as if begging. "Please, oh, please, Garnet. Fergus and Jon are entering. So are Orla and Nula."

She stood. "I suppose so, but it's against my better judgment."

"Yay." Hyacinth clapped her hands.

Joey took her hand. "Come on, let's go get ready."

The two ran ahead.

Garnet called, "Children, wait for us."

Adam called, "Joey, Hyacinth, stay with us." He grabbed Garnet's hand. "Come on, I've lost sight of them."

They threaded their way through the crowd.

They reached the start of the three-legged race. Children were lining up at the start line.

Garnet searched each direction. Panic rose in her throat. "I don't see them."

"I don't either. Let's ask the man running the contest."

Garnet tugged his hand. "Mr. Reilly, have you seen my niece and nephew?"

He peered around. "They were right here not five seconds ago but I don't see them now."

Tommy Bridges stopped wrapping his leg to that of Sean and turned to Garnet. "I saw them. They went with that man who said he was your cousin. They didn't look happy."

Garnet sank to her knees. "Dear merciful heaven, Frank has them." She wanted to curl into a ball and weep. She couldn't give in to her fright. What She had to do was find her children.

Adam lifted her up and supported her. "Tommy, which way did they go?"

He pointed. "Down to the end of the block and then they turned north."

"Tommy, Sean, this is real important or I wouldn't ask you to skip the race. The man who took them is a killer. I need for you to find the marshal or the sheriff and tell whichever one you find what you just told me. Tell them Frank Lawson has Joey and Hyacinth Chandler. Frank Lawson, got that? My wife and I are going to the café kitchen to see if there's been a ransom note."

He placed an arm around her shoulders. "Come on, honey, we have to get back to the café. He may have left a note for you. You can do it, put one foot in front of the other."

Tears fell from her eyes. "I will, Adam. Oh, no, what will Eunice and Harold say? They'll never agree to leave the children here now."

He shepherded her toward the café. "Don't think about that now. First I have to find them and bring them home."

When they reached the café's back door, they found a piece of paper wedged in the door.

Garnet grabbed the note. "Open the door, so we can see what it says."

GARNET

Someone had left a lamp burning on the table. Garnet and Adam rushed to the light.

Bring the jewelry to the old mine or the kids die. Be quick. If you're not here by midnight, they're dead.

She sank onto a seat. "It's in Wells Fargo's safe except for the pieces I promised you for helping me."

"Maybe that's all we'll need. Are the others in a case, a box, what?"

"They were in Great-Gran's jewelry box, which is in delicate condition. I-I kept the box and put the jewels in a small purse."

"Get the box and the pieces you saved out. Are you able to do that? If not, tell me where they are and I'll get them."

Cordelia and Aubrey rushed in the kitchen.

"You have a ransom demand." Aubrey grabbed the note.

Cordelia patted Garnet on the shoulder. "Doc Spense is on his way. He'll give you something to calm you."

"I don't want to be calmed. I want my children."

Adam knelt in front of her and took her hands. "Tell me where the box and the pieces you saved are."

"In the chest of drawers but I'll come with you. I'll have to tell Eunice and Harold something."

She rose but leaned heavily on Adam. "How difficult it must be to always have to be strong like you are."

"You're always strong. Just hold on for a few more hours."

Chapter Nineteen

In their bedroom, Adam guided her to the chest. She opened a drawer and took out an aged jewelry box. Inside were the brooch and bracelet she'd saved for him.

He took them from her. "Will you wait here and rest?"

"You know the answer to that. Frank will expect me to come."

When they were in the hallway, Eunice and Harold came out of their bedroom.

Eunice hurried forward. "What's happened? What's all the commotion downstairs in the kitchen?"

"There's no good way to say this. The children have been kidnapped."

"What are you doing here then?" Harold demanded.

Eunice started sobbing. "Those poor children. They'll be so scared."

Adam guided Garnet toward the stairs. "The county sheriff and town marshal are downstairs. We came back here to see if there had been a ransom demand and there had been. Garnet had the ransom—at least the part we're taking—in our room."

Harold motioned them ahead. "We'll follow you to the kitchen."

They went to the kitchen table and Garnet sat before she collapsed. Eunice and Harold also took a seat.

Aubrey had unrolled a map and had it spread on the table. He and the marshal leaned over it. "Cordelia and I can stay hidden here." He tapped the map.

Harold slapped a hand on the table. "I'll go along."

Aubrey sent Harold a glare. "No, just us four—Garnet, Adam, Cordelia, and me. More than that might cause Lawson to do something foolish."

GARNET

Garnet used a handkerchief to dry her tears. "Frank has a terrible temper. I think he's insane."

Adam stood behind her, soothing her by rubbing her shoulders. "He must be mad to have done the things he has. Don't worry, honey, we'll get our children back."

Aubrey rolled up the map. "Bundle up. We'll go to the livery and get horses. Garnet, can you ride?"

"Yes, and not just sidesaddle."

The timbre of Adam's voice changed. "Each of us needs a lantern. We'll also need a rope to tie up the men we capture."

Garnet knew his mind was at the mine, already plotting this fight. She held tight to the jewelry box. Yearning to hold the children almost defeated her.

Adam clapped Harold on the back. "We leave you two in charge. People may stop by to inquire about the kidnapping. I don't think there'll be another ransom demand, but we can't be sure."

"Eunice and I will keep watch." Harold nodded goodbye to those leaving.

The four strode quickly to the livery. Jasper Jones helped saddle and bridle the horses he'd chosen. When they'd mounted, they headed for the mine.

Garnet wasn't dressed to ride astride. She tried in vain to adjust her skirt so her ankles and calves didn't show. She soon gave it up as unimportant when the children's lives were at stake.

Cordelia visibly shuddered. "This brings back bad memories of the mine disaster. I've avoided this place."

Aubrey patted Cordelia's arm. "No wonder. You can go back if this is too hard for you. We'll understand completely."

She had a disgusted expression on her face. "I'll do my job same as you do yours."

Eerie silence engulfed them. The Harvest Moon cast golden light. Even the predators like wolves and wildcats were quiet tonight.

As they approached the old mine, Aubrey held up his hand. "We'll tie the horses here and go the rest of the way on foot."

Adam helped Garnet. "He's bound to have heard us approach. I haven't spotted a lookout."

"Neither have I. The mine opening is over here." Aubrey turned toward a dark patch on the landscape.

Cordelia warned, "A gunshot inside the tunnel is likely to cause another disaster."

Garnet summoned all her fortitude to step to the mouth of the tunnel. She imagined Cordelia was suffering from the same memories as she.

Pointing his revolver at them, Frank called, "That's far enough. Let's see the jewelry."

Adam took the box from Garnet and held it so the lantern illuminated it. "I have it here. Let's see the children."

Frank reached to the side and grabbed Joey and Hyacinth. He shoved them in front of him.

Hyacinth was sobbing. "I want Garnet. I want her to take us home with Adam."

Joey's lips trembled, but he wasn't crying. "See, she and Adam are here like I said, sister, and we can go home in a few minutes."

Frank yelled. "I told you brats to keep quiet."

Joey and Hyacinth winced. Garnet wanted to rush Frank and pummel him hard then shoot him. Then stomp on him.

Beside her, Adam stiffened. "Send them over here if you want the box." He was inching forward by moving as if he were shifting his weight.

Frank held Hyacinth by her braid. "How do I know it's not empty? Let's see some proof."

Adam opened the box so only he could see inside and then held up the brooch. "This what you wanted?"

Frank licked his lips. "Maybe the box is empty now."

Garnet warned quietly, "Frank's planning something to double cross us. Hear how his voice changed?"

Just as quietly, Adam agreed, "I noticed. Be ready to run."

Adam opened the box and took out the bracelet. He dangled it on his finger. "This proves this box is the one Great Gran gave Garnet. If you want it, send me the children."

Frank stayed where he was, gun in one hand and the other on Hyacinth's head. His evil grin sent chills up Garnet's spine.

"You bring the box here."

Adam smiled as if this were a pleasant day's outing. "Glad to, but I won't hand it over until I have the children."

Frank released Hyacinth and stuck out his hand to receive the jewelry box.

Adam lunged for the children and shoved the box at Frank. "Run!"

Adam scooped up the children and ran. Frank fired at him and missed.

A horrendous boom shook the earth and the tunnel fell into the abyss. Garnet felt the earth falling away beneath her as she ran. She turned to see Adam and the children.

Cordelia grabbed her hand and tugged her with Cordelia and Aubrey. She looked over her shoulder.

Adam tossed the children towards her. They ran the rest of the way. The ground beneath Adam crumbled until he dropped from sight and only his fingers showed.

"Adam!" She edged toward him.

"Stay back, I'll pull you down if you try to help. Get the rope. Hurry, I can't hold on much longer."

Aubrey ran up with the rope and looped it around Adam's arms. He and Cordelia and Garnet pulled. The edge of the cave-in crumbled and spread as they worked. The hole was like a great vortex growing wider and wider.

They appeared to be making no headway as they backed up further and further. Adam's weight crumbled the crater's edge. Finally, Adam inched his body upward little by little until he was on solid ground. He rolled free of the pit, sat up, and removed the rope.

Both children threw themselves at him. Garnet joined the children in embracing Adam. For a few minutes, she thought they'd lost him.

Joey hugged him. "I knew you'd come get us."

Dust created by the cave-in had turned the tears on Hyacinth's face into muddy tracks. "He did, Adam, he told me you'd come. That mean man said if you did he'd kill you and Garnet. I was sure scared."

Garnet hugged all three of them. "I was scared, too. I can't be without my family."

GARNET

Chapter Twenty

Adam stood and dusted himself off. "Sorry about your family jewelry box, Garnett. I couldn't find a way to save it."

He reached into his pocket and pulled out the brooch and bracelet. "I saved these for you."

She gasped. "I was positive you put those back into the box."

"I hoped that's what Frank would think. Apparently he did." He walked toward Aubrey with his hand outstretched. "Thanks for saving me. No need for a trial for Lawson and his buddies."

The sheriff shook Adam's hand. "Saves money and trouble. He can't break out where he is."

Aubrey knelt in front of the children. "Were there other men in there as well as the one who spoke with Adam?"

Joey wouldn't let go of Garnet's hand. "There were two. They were mean-looking but they didn't hurt us. They just did whatever that Frank said. He acted crazy, always having temper tantrums over nothing."

Hyacinth nodded. "Frank hit Joey 'cause brother was protecting me." She sniffled. "I was scared and couldn't stop crying."

Garnet hugged the little girl. "Of course not. That was a frightening experience that would make a grown up cry. I hope nothing that bad ever happens again."

Garnet hugged Cordelia. "Thank you for putting duty above what must have brought back painful memories. I'm sorry you had to come here."

Cordelia's eyes were moist but she put up a brave front. "I'm the marshal and I perform my job as well as possible. I certainly wasn't going to abandon you or these children."

As her friend spoke, Garnet thought about the Millers. They had the ammunition they needed to say she was unfit to raise the children. What were they thinking even now?

Adam lifted Hyacinth. "Let's go home."

Aubrey twined his fingers with Cordelia's. "Sounds like a fine idea. Bennett, I'll see you get your reward for the three men. We won't try to recover their bodies. Too dangerous."

Cordelia turned to him. "You'd better believe that, Aubrey Bowles. The edge of that hole may crumble more. Someone needs to build a fence around there so no one accidentally falls into the crater."

Aubrey sent her a weary smile. "Good idea. We don't want any of the local daredevils going there. That's the kind of thing teen-aged boys would do for adventure."

They mounted their horses. Hyacinth rode with Garnet and Joey rode with Adam.

He led the way toward town. "When it's daylight, I'll come back to find the horses. I don't know if any of my gear is still with my mule, but I hope so."

Aubrey rode alongside Adam. "I'll come with you tomorrow morning. Not too early."

"That sounds about right. About ten good for you?"

"I'll be at the café at ten." He kneed his horse and led Cordelia toward town at a lope.

With the children riding double, Garnet and Adam rode slower. By the time they turned in the horses at the livery and carried the children home, the time was after midnight.

The Millers had left a note propped on the table and anchored by the salt shaker. Adam picked it up and handed it to Garnet. Heads together, they read it.

Doctor sedated Eunice. Hope you've got the children with you safe and sound. Front door is locked and I put a sign on the door that says Closed For Family Emergency so you don't have to worry about the breakfast crowd tomorrow.
HM

Adam carried Joey but locked the back door. "Let's get the kids to bed. They can clean up in the morning."

GARNET

Garnet hugged a sleeping Hyacinth to her. "I can make it up the stairs but not much farther. Bed will feel good."

Harold poked his head out of the bedroom. "Thanks be to God for His mercy, you have the children. You can tell me about it at breakfast." He retreated and closed the door.

When they'd tucked in the children, Garnet and Adam went to their bedroom. She removed her half boots and crawled under the cover fully clothed. "I'm too tired to undress."

"I'm too dusty not to shed these clothes." She heard him stripping but was asleep before he came to bed.

Usually, Garnet rose at half past five. This morning, the sun was up when she woke. "I've overslept."

Adam shoved his shirttail into his britches. "Doesn't matter. By now everyone in town knows what happened. Harold left that sign on the door so you're covered."

Garnet had never had a hangover but she thought this must be what one was like. Her head pounded and she ached everywhere, making her uncharacteristically grumpy. "Adam, of course it matters. There are a lot of strangers in town who have to eat somewhere. I'm losing money, money I'll need to get through the winter."

"You're not a work horse and you needed rest. What's done is done."

Garnet sighed. "Sorry I snapped. We've both forgotten that this is Sunday and I'm always closed."

She put her hands on her cheeks. "I'm so worried about what the Millers will say. We'll have to go to court to get custody for sure. You know they'll blame me for this. They'll be right, too."

"Lawson was a greedy killer. How is that your fault? No one could place this at your door."

"I was in charge of the children and I let them out of my sight. That's how I'm to blame."

"You can't be with them day and night. You can't keep them in their rooms like a prison, either." He opened the bedroom door.

Hyacinth and Joey were standing where they'd been waiting.

Garnet's niece hugged her legs. "Joey said I couldn't bother you. Grandma said I hafta take a bath. Do I?"

After lifting the little girl to her arms, Garnet hugged her. "Yes, dear, you need a bath." She looked at her nephew. "You do, too, Joey."

"I figured but I don't care because I'm home with you and Adam."

Garnet's heart pounded so hard she thought Adam must hear. Now that Frank was no longer on the loose, Adam had no reason to stay. She held her breath, willing him to answer that he would remain here with them. She was disappointed.

Adam ruffled Joey's hair as they headed toward the stairs. "That you are. Hope you're recovering from your ordeal this morning."

Joey was solemn. "I won't ever forget that man grabbing us, but I knew I could depend on you two to rescue Hyacinth and me. I was sure scared that Frank might shoot you, though."

Garnet had feared the same thing.

In the kitchen, Adam grabbed a cup. "Coffee sure smells good. Glad you started it, Eunice."

Eunice tentatively smiled. "I thought we could all use some first thing this morning. You two sit at the table and I'll make ham and eggs. My biscuits aren't as fluffy as Garnet's but they'll do."

Garnet couldn't believe her ears. She was still shaky and was willing to sit and hold Hyacinth. Good heavens, the clock displayed eight o'clock. She couldn't remember when she'd slept this late.

Adam sat with his legs outstretched until Joey climbed onto his lap. "We missed supper yesterday. I wonder if the rest of you are as hungry as I am."

Harold rubbed his belly. "I figure I can afford to skip a meal or two. In spite of that, I'm looking forward to a big breakfast.

Despair wrapped around Garnet. Regardless of what Adam did, she could not lose these precious children. She dreaded a court battle. If Adam left, what chance would she have to win? None, that's what.

Her niece threw her arms around Garnet's neck. "I'm sure glad Joey and I have you and Adam. We're a nice family, aren't we?"

Garnet hugged Hyacinth to her. "The nicest."

Harold looked at his granddaughter. "Nicer than your mother, Hyacinth?"

The little girl looked at him. "Different. Garnet said we can't ever forget our real mama and papa. She hung a picture in my room and one in Joey's to help us remember."

Joey turned to look at his grandfather. "Adam spends more time with us than Papa did. Papa had to work in the mine all day. He didn't get to see us much except on Sunday. Adam is here every day and talks to us and plays games with us. He's even nice to our friends."

Adam looked at Joey as if perplexed. "Of course I am. You're a special boy and girl and they're your friends. That makes them welcome here."

Eunice served breakfast. "The range here sure is a nice one."

Garnet took a slice of ham from the platter. "I agree. I love having hot water available.

The children brought the butter and jam to the table. They talked about the festival while they ate. Apparently no one wanted to relive the horror of the kidnapping.

Aubrey arrived as they were finishing their meal. "Sorry, I'm a little early."

Eunice asked, "Have you had breakfast, sheriff?"

"Yes, ma'am, but thank you. Bennett, you ready to go?"

"I am." He stood. "We're going to find the horses those men used. We can't leave them tied or hobbled somewhere with no food or water and no defense against predators."

Joey grabbed Adam's sleeve. "Can I come?"

"You promise to do exactly what I say?"

The little boy crossed his heart. "I will, I promise."

Garnet's temper flared. "Adam, he needs to stay here. He's too young to go out like that."

Adam took her hand and knelt in front of her. "Honey, Joey needs to go back there to conquer his fear. I know you're especially good with the children, but I was a little boy and I know this. Going back up there right away is the only way he'll heal from what happened."

"You should have asked me before you asked him. We should have talked it over."

He brushed tendrils of hair from her face. "You're right and I apologize. I'll remember in the future."

She sighed. "You'd better make sure he doesn't get hurt." Did in the future mean he planned to be here?

Joey jumped up and down. "Yay, I get to go on a horse."

Hyacinth patted Garnet's face. "I don't want to go. That horse was bumpy."

"Thank you for staying here with your grandparents and me. We'd be lonely if both you and Joey went with Adam."

Eunice grabbed Garnet's hand. "We'd like to know what happened and how it all came about."

"You deserve to know. Hyacinth, why don't you go get Molly while I talk to your grandparents? I'll bet you need to tell her what happened."

The little girl's eyes widened. "I do. I'll bet she worried about me." She ran up the stairs.

Garnet explained about the jewelry and Frank's obsession with it. While she was confessing, she included why Adam had stayed there.

Harold appeared disapproving. "You mean you're not really married?"

Garnet held up a hand. "Oh, yes, we're married. Adam's been wonderful about helping me. The children adore him. What I wanted you to understand is that he came here to find Frank Lawson, the man who kidnapped the children. When Frank broke out of prison, he killed a friend of Adam's from Army days."

GARNET

Chapter Twenty-One

Adam kept scanning the area as they rode. That and making sure Joey didn't fall off his horse. To be sure, Adam held the reins for now. Joey appeared content to hold on to the pommel.

The three of them circled the old mine. By day, the sight of that gaping hole was frightening. How he'd survived was a miracle. Chills ran up his spine. He almost hadn't come out of that alive.

They widened their circle until they sighted the camp. His tent was set up and the horses hobbled between two trees. Adam tied up his rented horse and helped Joey to the ground. "Come on, son, and meet my horse, Brandy."

"Hello, old boy. How have you been treated?" Adam examined the horse, looking for sores or pulled muscles. The horse nuzzled him as if happy to see him.

"He sure is a pretty horse." Joey petted Brandy's nose.

A loud bray made Adam laugh. "Come on, Joey, and I'll introduce you to the orneriest mule alive."

He strode to the animal. "I'm not forgetting you, Mossy. Sure glad to see you. How are you?" While he checked the mule, Mossy chattered at him.

Joey laughed. "Mossy sounds like he's scolding you for letting those men steal him."

"I'm sure he is. He has an opinion about everything."

Adam was sure happy to see his saddlebags. He examined the contents. Clothes were missing, but he didn't care about those. His papers and mementos were there.

Aubrey called, "You know if the horses stolen from your friend are among these?"

Adam strode to them. "These two on the end. See the _LF_ brand?"

"Yep. Found old letters with what I guess are the names of the two helping Lawson. Match up to the wanted posters."

Adam kept searching. "I found my rifle inside the tent, but don't see my Colt. You come across one?"

Aubrey shook his head. "Naw, you might as well keep the one Cordelia gave you. Looks like a pretty good rig and whoever it once belonged to must be either dead or in prison."

"Found my papers. Food's gone, but most of the gear is here. Sure glad to have my animals and saddles back."

They'd brought oats for the horses and Mossy. Once they animals had a chance to eat, he led them to a stream nearby. After they'd drunk and were back in camp, he saddled Brandy.

Adam felt Joey's eyes on his every move.

Joey asked, "Will I get a horse someday?"

Adam was not getting caught in Garnet's crosshairs again. "I'll have to talk that over with Garnet, but I imagine so. You'll have to be old enough to care for the horse as well as ride. A man needs a horse out here but they're a big responsibility."

He collapsed the tent and stowed it on Mossy, along with camping gear and bedroll. After covering the pack with a tarp, he secured the load.

"Joey, I'll help you mount." He didn't know how he was going to lead four animals and keep tabs on Joey. He tied the reins of Joey's horse to Mossy's pack. The last thing the mule would do was bolt and run. He tied the horses in tandem them mounted Brandy.

"Sure feels good to be in my saddle on my horse."

Aubrey led the two criminals' horses and tied their reins to his saddle. "What will you do about your friend's horses?" He mounted his horse.

"What do you suggest? Lance didn't have any family but had hoped to marry soon as he found a wife."

"Then I reckon they're yours unless you want to donate them to the town or county."

"If you think it'll be okay, I'd like to keep them. Lance was a good friend. I don't think he'd mind."

"Shouldn't since you tracked the man who killed him. Not much consolation for your friend, but justice in the broader sense."

"Sometimes that's all we have, isn't it?"

"And, sometimes, not even that."

***

When she'd finished explaining about Frank to the Millers, she called to her niece, "Hyacinth, you should have your bath before lunch." To her guests, she said, "Will you excuse me? I need to hurry so I can finish preparing our noon meal."

Eunice asked, "Can I give her a bath? It's been so long since I bathed Desdemona."

"If you wish. I'll get her fresh clothes."

Hyacinth skipped to the bathing room. "Don't forget my bath time things."

Garnet rolled her eyes, wondering if Eunice realized what her granddaughter's baths involved. She gathered the clean clothes as well as the toys she wanted in the tub with her. Along the way, she grabbed a stool for Eunice to sit on while she helped Hyacinth.

"Remember, there's only enough hot water for a few inches in the tub. Don't try to talk Grandma into more."

"Oka-a-a-y. Grandma, in summer I get to have the tub half full so I can play swim."

Garnet opened a cupboard. "Here's a towel and washcloth. Eunice, do you want me to stay and help or do you want to do this solo?"

"Let me do it on my own."

"Call out if you need me." Garnet didn't know whether to go downstairs or wait nearby. She decided Eunice had survived bathing three children and could tackle one little girl of six.

Maybe.

Garnet recalled the scars on Dessie's back. She had trouble visualizing the couple she'd come to know indulging in that inhumane behavior. Nevertheless, she'd seen the scars when she'd helped nurse Dessie during a bout of influenza.

With a sigh, Garnet went to the kitchen to prepare lunch. She'd already put the roast in the oven, usual Sunday fare because it cooked while they attended church.

She was setting the table when she heard a screech.

Hyacinth cried, "Garnet, Grandma fell."

GARNET

Chapter Twenty Two

Garnet raced up the stairs. When she reached the bathing room, Howard was helping Eunice to her feet.

Water pooled on the floor and Eunice's dress had wet splotches, to say nothing of the back where she'd sat on the floor.

"I'm all right." She shook free from Harold's hands then grabbed his arm to steady herself. "Hyacinth Chandler, you are a spoiled child."

Eunice glared at Garnet. "Does she make this much of a mess when you bathe her?"

Garnet shook her head. "Never. Hyacinth, what on earth caused so much water on the floor?"

"Grandma combed my hair while I was in the tub. She pulled and it hurt." She looked down. "I musta splashed."

Harold shook his finger at the little girl. "You need your hide tanned, young lady."

Garnet wrapped a towel around Hyacinth and lifted her. "No child needs his hide tanned. I saw the scars on Dessie's back. Anyone who treats a child like that needs to be horsewhipped." She grabbed the clean clothes, turned, and marched to Hyacinth's room.

She dried her niece and helped her dress. With a gentle hand, she combed tangles from Hyacinth's hair. "You were rude to Grandma. Plus, she could have really hurt herself from slipping on the wet floor. What if there was so much water it ruined the ceiling downstairs?"

"I'm sorry." Hyacinth crossed her arms. "I don't like her taking care of me. Garnet, I want you."

"People don't always get what they want, dear. You will stay in your room until I say you can come out. I'll go clean up your mess."

Near tears, she feared what this had done to the chances of keeping the children. The entire weekend had been one disaster after another.

She carried the towel back to the bathing room and mopped up the water on the floor. After pulling the plug from the drain, she collected the toys her niece enjoyed having in the tub. She wrung out the towel and hung it over the rim to dry.

Hyacinth was a little spoiled, but Garnet thought that was a good thing. Dessie and Joe had started her that way and Garnet had continued. In her opinion, every child needed to feel special, especially one whose world had collapsed.

Adam had spoiled Garnet. Even though theirs wasn't a true marriage as far as intimate relations, in other ways it was more real than hers had been with Michael. She wished Adam would come home and tell her he was staying.

She set the toys on the shelf in Hyacinth's room.

Her niece sat on her bed. "Can I come out yet?"

"Not until I say so. You play in here and think about how to be a good girl."

Garnet went down to the kitchen and finished preparing the noon meal. When it was ready to eat, she took a plate to her niece. "You eat in here. I don't think Grandpa and Grandma want to see you right now."

She walked down the hall and knocked on the Millers' door. "Dinner is ready." Without waiting for them, she returned to the kitchen. They could come or not, she didn't care.

She sat at the table. When the two guests came downstairs both looked sheep-faced. They took their seats.

"Since Adam isn't here, I'll say grace."

Dear Heavenly Father, hallowed by Thy name. Thank you for delivering Hyacinth and Joey from an evil man and preserving Adam's life. Bless those who are about to partake of this nourishment and those of this household who are absent from this table. Amen.

After they'd eaten in silence for a few minutes, Eunice cleared her throat. "I'd forgotten how demanding caring for a small child can be. All the bending and stooping is tiring."

Garnet wasn't buying that excuse. "I've always believed Hyacinth and Joey were easily cared for compared to other children."

Harold harrumphed. "They're spoiled."

"What would you have them do? Be seen but not heard? No playing on Sunday? No laughing, no joy? Is that your opinion of the correct way to raise a child?"

Harold pointed his fork at her. "We know our Christian duty. 'Spare the rod and spoil the child' is what the Bible says."

"It also says 'suffer the little children to come unto me for theirs is the kingdom of heaven.' Don't you quote things out of context, Harold Miller. I know the Bible as well or better than you do. Nowhere in the Bible does it say to be cruel to children."

Harold sent her a surly glare before he turned his attention to his food. As soon as the meal was over, Eunice helped clear the table.

Garnet regretted the whole bath episode. "Were you injured when you fell?"

"I'm sure I'll be sore tomorrow but there's no permanent damage done. The experience reminded me I'm twenty five years older than when Dessie was Hyacinth's age."

"Why don't you go up and rest and I'll finish the dishes."

Eunice dried her hands on a towel. "If you're sure you don't mind, I'm still tired from that sedative."

Garnet quickly finished cleaning the kitchen. She didn't want to go to the parlor and talk to Harold. There was no mending waiting and she'd finished Hyacinth's sweater. Besides, her knitting was in the parlor. The only outlet left for her nervous energy was to bake.

***

Once they were at the livery, Adam arranged to keep his horses and mule there and store his camping gear. He took his saddlebags and rifle with him and he and Joey walked back to the café.

He arrived to find Garnet seated in the kitchen munching on a cookie.

"Smells good in here. Why aren't you in the parlor or resting?"

"You missed lunch but I saved you each a plate." She rose and walked to the range. "Eunice is resting."

She turned back and tried to make light of the situation. "She wanted to give Hyacinth a bath. I think she'd forgotten how fussy her granddaughter is about everything being just so. I guess Harold is reading. Someone gave him a Denver paper. He took it up with him."

When the two males were eating, she filled them in on the whole bath debacle. "Hyacinth is probably asleep. I made her eat in her room."

Adam dug into his food. "Raising kids is work, even good kids like Joey and Hyacinth."

"I suppose but I've never considered them work. They require extra time and supervision, but I enjoy them."

Joey swallowed. "Thanks, Garnet. We like being with you and Adam. Can I go upstairs now?"

"You need a bath. I'll be up in a few minutes. I want to talk to Adam a bit first."

Joey went upstairs.

Tears welled in her eyes. "Oh, Adam, what will I do if I lose them?"

He stood and pulled her into his embrace. "Honey, their grandparents got a taste of what caring for children can be. They needed that dose of reality to show them they're not as young as they were when their children were this age."

She buried her face against his broad chest. "Eunice mentioned she realized that fact even though she thinks the children are spoiled. Harold thinks Joey and Hyacinth need to have their hides tanned."

"He'd better not try in front of me is all I can say."

She raised her head. "Thank you. Talking with you always makes me feel better."

"Come on, let's go up there." Holding her hand, he led her to the stairs.

In the parlor, Joey was telling his grandfather about finding the camp and animals.

Harold held his paper. "You liked riding a horse, did you?"

"I did but Adam kept the reins in case something scared the horse. I held on to the pom… pommel. We brought Brandy and Mossy and two other horses to the livery."

Harold raised his eyebrows. "Is one of them going to be your horse?"

Joey shook his head. "Naw, horses are a big respon'bility. I'll have to know how to take care of one before I can own one. Adam said he and Garnet have to talk and I'll have to be a little older."

Harold chuckled and looked at Adam. "Learned that lesson, did you?"

Adam laughed. "Sure did. Not making promises unless Garnet and I discuss the matter first."

Garnet felt the heat from a blush spread across her face. "Joey, you need a bath."

Adam stood. "I'll supervise then it's my turn. We both smell like horses, right, Joey? I'm surprised your aunt let us inside the building."

Joey laughed at Adam's comment.

She really couldn't be civil to Harold right now. "If you'll excuse me, Harold, I'm still overtired from the stress of yesterday. I'm going to lie down a while."

Chapter Twenty Three

That night in their room, Garnet crawled under the cover. "They asked for a detailed explanation of what happened yesterday. I wish I hadn't now but I confessed you'd come here to get Frank."

"Nothing wrong with that. Hyacinth's bath sounds like a major debacle."

She snapped to defend herself, "It was but that's not all my fault. Harold was out of line."

He slid between the covers. "Hey, I didn't blame you."

"Sorry. Guess I'm feeling guilty. You know I have a temper but I usually do a better job of controlling myself. Oh, Adam, think how hard Dessie must have been whipped as a child to still have scars as an adult."

"Bad enough he treated her like that. Now I know he'd do the same to Hyacinth and Joey, I'll find it hard to be civil to him. Makes me wonder if he's treated Eunice the same way. There ought to be laws protecting children and wives."

"Oh, I hadn't considered his treatment of Eunice. If his temper is that harsh, he probably has taken it out on her too."

"I've no respect for a man who hits a woman or a child. I don't mean a light spanking to a child where there's no physical damage. Still, we don't punish Joey or Hyacinth that way."

"They were already trained when I met them. I've merely continued as their parents had. Joe worked such long hours, mostly Dessie cared for them."

Adam laid an arm across her waist and kissed her temple. "Don't worry any more. We'll keep them. Snuggle down and get some sleep. Café opens early."

***

GARNET

Monday Garnet was busy. Some people who'd come for the Harvest Festival had stayed over until today. She was grateful for the extra customers.

Being so rushed left no time to worry about Eunice and Harold. The children were in school and Adam helped her. The Millers were left to entertain themselves on their own.

On one trip to the kitchen, Garnet stopped to talk to Adam. "I saw the Millers walk in front of the café. Do you know where they were going?"

He flipped a steak in the skillet. "Not a clue. You've kept me so busy I hardly spoke to them. After you told me Harold thought Hyacinth needed her hide tanned, I've had to force myself to be civil. I hope they stay gone all day."

They didn't but it was evening before Garnet and Adam had time to share a conversation with the Millers. They sat at the kitchen table after the café closed.

Joey worked on his times tables while Hyacinth practiced printing her letters.

Joey looked at Adam. "You think it's gonna snow soon?"

He nodded. "I do. If we don't have a blizzard by the end of the week, I'll be surprised."

Eunice sent Harold a glance. "I hope snow doesn't arrive before Wednesday. That's when we're leaving."

Garnet set slices of apple pie for each person. "There won't be enough to prevent your trip. You only have to get to Curdys Crossing to reach the rail lines."

Harold laid a hand on Joey's shoulder. "You have a suitcase for the trip?"

Joey shook his head. "Grandpa, Garnet said I have to respect you and Grandma but I'm not going to live with you. Hyacinth and I want to stay with Garnet and Adam."

His grandfather frowned. "Don't you know children do as they're told?"

"I do what Garnet and Adam tell me." He looked at Garnet. "I'm trying not to be rude, Garnet, but I want to stay with you."

Seated on Joey's other side, Adam laid his hand on Joey's back. "You're staying here. Remember, we told you Garnet talked to an important lawyer."

Her nephew smiled. "I didn't forget. When Grandpa and Grandma talk like we have to go with them, it scares me."

Eunice reached across the table to squeeze Joey's hand. "We don't want to scare you. Why does the thought of going to live with Grandpa and me frighten you?"

Joey laid his pencil on the paper. "Mama talked about growing up with you. She told me things you did to punish her and what she'd done to deserve it."

The boy shook his head. "Mama was right. It was too much for a little girl. She didn't want to visit you. We only came because she wanted to say goodbye to her Grandma."

"Our own daughter didn't want to visit us?" Eunice took out her handkerchief and dabbed at her eyes. "Did you hear that, Harold?"

He slumped in his chair. "I did but I don't understand. We did our best raising our three but none of them wants to be around us. We gave them a good home with all they needed. They're ungrateful."

Garnet couldn't help sympathy for the couple, misguided as they were. "You left out several ingredients."

Harold snapped, "Such as?"

Garnet looked from Eunice to Harold. "Compassion, joy, and love."

Eunice leaned forward. "I'll have you know we love each of our children."

Adam asked, "How often have you told them? How do you show your love?"

Eunice spluttered, "I don't have to tell them. Mothers love their children, they know that. We showed our love by providing them with food and clothing and a safe place to live."

Garnet held out both hands. "The point of this discussion is to tell you that Adam and I will go to court if necessary in order to insure we have custody of Joey and Hyacinth."

Harold stood. "I don't have to listen to this. Eunice, are you coming?"

GARNET

His wife rose slowly. "Yes, Harold, I'm coming with you. Maybe that's part of the problem—I always follow your lead." She nodded and turned to walk to the stairs.

Garnet put her elbows on the table and cradled her head in her hands. "That was unpleasant. Tomorrow is the last day they'll be here. We should try to keep it as pleasant as possible."

Joey looked up. "But we won't have to go with them, will we?"

She shook her head. "No, dear. You and Hyacinth will stay here with Adam and me. Right now, it's time for two children I know to get in bed."

Hyacinth stood. "You'll read us a story, won't you?"

"I'll be up in a few minutes and will read to you."

When the children had climbed the stairs, Garnet turned to Adam. "We didn't settle matters. If anything, all we did was generate animosity. I dread tomorrow and until the stage leaves Wednesday."

"Everything will work out all right. Eunice and Harold have to realize you and I can do a better job raising Hyacinth and Joey than they can. In the meantime, let's go put the kids to bed."

CAROLINE CLEMMONS

Chapter Twenty Four

Breakfast began with the Millers' silence. Adam joked with the children and kept the conversation going. Garnet admired the way he acted with her niece and nephew. "Whose turn to turn the sign to *Open*?"

"Mine." Hyacinth raced to the dining room.

Garnet tilted her head. "Wasn't it her turn last time?"

Joey grinned. "Yeah, but she likes to so much I let her have extra turns."

Garnet hugged him. "You are such a wonderful boy."

She had food going by the time the bell over the front door dinged that the first diner had arrived.

When she returned to the kitchen, Garnet carried the coffeepot. "Would you care for more coffee?" She hovered the coffeepot over Harold's cup.

"Thank you." He pushed his empty breakfast plate away. Good meal and I'm stuffed."

Eunice cleared her throat and sent her husband a meaningful stare.

Harold tugged at his ear lobe. "Yes, well, my wife and I talked things over. Frankly, she talked and I listened but she convinced me. We believe you two will make the best guardians for our grandchildren."

Euphoria filled Garnet. "Thank you. You've made the right decision."

Adam shook Harold's hand. "Indeed you have. You won't regret your choice. You have my word on that."

Joey and Hyacinth cheered and hugged Garnet.

Her nephew pulled away and looked at his grandparents. "We don't want to hurt your feelings or be rude, Grandma and Grandpa. We really like living with Garnet and Adam."

GARNET

Garnet had been in and out of the kitchen while Adam manned the range.

She laid a hand on the head of each child. "Time for school. There's a cold wind today so be sure you wear your hats."

Hyacinth pouted. "That old hat musses my hair."

Adam tugged at her curls. "Princess Hyacinth, you don't want to be sick." He picked her up and tickled her stomach. "You could catch something that would make your hair fall out."

She giggled. "Okay, I'll wear that hat."

He set Hyacinth on the floor then Adam laid his hand on Joey's shoulder. "When you get home from school, do you want to go with me to check on the horses and Mossy?"

Joey's eyes lit up. Not just his eyes. His entire face beamed. "Can I? That'd be great."

"I'll wait until you're here before I go check on them."

The children left for school.

During her between-meal slow down, Garnet sat at the table.

Harold looked at her. "I'm concerned about your life when you're snowed in this winter. How will you survive?"

Garnet met his gaze. "I have some savings put by for the winter months but we have simple needs. The main thing I have to buy is coal. I've already stocked up on that and have enough for a year."

She peeked into the dining room to check on customers then returned to the table. "We have plenty of food and get beef and swine year round from the nearby Rafter O Ranch. Our winter clothes are warm. I'll only serve breakfast and lunch. With the extra time, we play games, read, knit and sew, and visit with one another in town."

Eunice surveyed the room. "This is more comfortable than I remembered from when we were here several years ago."

Garnet assessed the kitchen. She loved this place. "Michael and his first wife spent her inheritance on this building. They weren't practical but his wife had excellent taste and expected quality. The children and I are reaping the rewards."

Adam ambled toward them then sat at the table. "Ahem, you forget me?"

Garnet smiled and caressed his arm. "Never. How could you think I'd forget you, Mr. Bennett?"

She hadn't included him because she believed he'd soon be leaving, especially since the Millers agreed not to fight for custody. She'd always be grateful to Adam. She dreaded the day he would leave.

She couldn't think about him going away on this day when she had so much for which to be grateful. Frank would never bother anyone again. The Millers weren't battling for custody. Adam didn't die when the crater opened. The children weren't physically harmed when they were kidnapped.

***

When time came for the Millers to catch the stage, the wind was bitter. Overhead the sky was steel gray.

Adam set a suitcase on the boardwalk near the stage and extended his hand to Harold. "Looks like you're leaving just in time to avoid being stuck here for the winter."

Harold shook Adam's hand. "Appreciate your hospitality but we're ready to go home."

"I understand. There's nothing better than being in your own bed at night."

Garnet handed them a basket. "This will feed you for a couple of days. If you don't run into trouble, that should get you home."

A wide smile graced Eunice's face. "Thank you. I don't like the stage or train stop food. This will be welcome."

Two men Adam didn't recognize climbed on top of the stage. He knew Ben was in charge of the Wells Fargo office and that's why he no longer rode shotgun.

The new driver leaned down. "Everyone who's riding with me, get aboard."

When the Millers and two other passengers were inside, the driver snapped the reins. "Yee Haw."

Adam stood with his arm around Garnet and waved at the departing stage. She fit perfectly in his arms. Keeping his hands—and other parts—to himself every night had been a test of his endurance.

Adam said, "Well, that's a chapter in our lives I'm not sorry to see end."

"I'm relieved but incredibly tired. Having them here took the starch out of me. Guess I'll go back inside to work."

Adam accompanied her. He'd seen Wells Fargo had received a canvas money bag. Surely his reward was included.

His future depended on that reward. He'd wasted too many years traveling hither and yon chasing ruthless men. When he'd said Lawson was his last chase, he'd been dead serious.

What would Garnet say when she learned his plans?

Chapter Twenty Five

Adam and Joey returned from the livery to find Aubrey and Cordelia waiting in the kitchen. That perked up Adam. He hung his coat and hat on a peg. Joey did the same.

"Cordelia, Aubrey, nice to see you. Did Garnet abandon you?"

The swinging door opened and she glided in. "I did and my backup helpers were also gone."

Cordelia waved a hand dismissively. "Folks come here to eat and you have to feed them. Besides, we came to see you, Adam."

Joey tugged on Adam's sleeve. "May I be excused to go to my room?"

"You may."

Joey ran up the stairs.

Adam chuckled. "He had to sleep on the parlor couch while his grandparents were here. Obviously, he's eager to get his room back the way he wants it."

"Don't blame him." Aubrey pulled an envelope out of his coat pocket. "I'd wired about you catching Lawson and his buddies. Reward came in on the stage. I figured you'd like to have it as soon as possible."

Adam accepted the envelope. He wouldn't insult the sheriff by counting it in his presence. Instead, he shoved it inside his pants pocket. He'd count it later.

"I appreciate it. Also appreciate knowing you two. Glad to meet honest law officers who are also nice people."

Garnet carried in a load of dirty dishes then came to the table. "Would you like a dish of peach cobbler?"

Cordelia groaned. "You know I can't resist your peach cobbler."

Aubrey chuckled. "I won't even try to refuse a portion."

Adam rose to help Garnet. When they'd all been served, he and Garnet sat at the table.

Cordelia spooned in a bite and closed her eyes. "You are the best cook I know, Garnet."

"Thank you. I hope to continue here for many years."

Aubrey swallowed. "You folks glad to be shed of the children's grandparents?"

Adam met his gaze. "I think 'glad' is an understatement. We've been walking on egg shells while they were here."

Garnet twirled her spoon. "I was afraid they'd get snowed in and we'd be stuck with them all winter. You'd have had to arrest me in that case because I'd have strangled Harold Miller."

Cordelia chuckled. "You don't have to worry about a custody trial, do you?"

Garnet shook her head. "No, they agreed Adam and I are a better bet as guardians."

"I think Hyacinth's bath on Sunday clinched it." Adam told them about the incident.

Aubrey and Cordelia laughed and laughed.

Cordelia caught her breath. "I think you exaggerated."

Garnet looked at Adam. "Unfortunately, he didn't. Although, I must admit he's better at telling stories than I am."

Adam stood and bowed to his wife. "Why, thank you, Mrs. Bennett." He picked up his bowl. "Anyone for seconds?"

Aubrey pushed his dish toward Adam. "I wouldn't turn one down."

Cordelia thought for a couple of seconds. "I can't refuse."

Garnet looked at Adam. "Why not just bring the pan of cobbler and serving spoon to the table? And the coffee pot."

After the children were tucked in that evening, Adam ushered Garnet to the parlor instead of downstairs.

"Now that we have the parlor to ourselves, let's enjoy the softer furniture."

She sat on the couch and yawned. "A good idea. I think it will take me a week to get over the fatigue of the kidnapping and the Millers."

Adam sat beside her. "At a minimum. I know you have to serve disagreeable people sometimes in the café. At least now we don't have to be around people we don't enjoy up here in our home." He hoped he could include himself in that scene.

She wrung her hands until he held them. "Adam, what do you plan to do now? Frank's no longer a threat and the Millers have gone."

"You eager to get rid of me?"

"No, of course not, quite the opposite. For one thing, the children adore you."

"I guess I'm more interested in how you feel about me." He twined his fingers with hers.

She half turned toward him. "Does that mean you're considering staying? That we'll be a real family?"

"Well, I have all this newfound wealth. Maybe not a lot of money for some, but a nice stake for me. I wired my brother to tell him he can buy my half of the ranch and that will increase my fortune. I thought I might buy interest in a business."

Her heart rate sped. "What kind of business?"

"I've recently learned I enjoy the café business. Do you know where I could buy a half-interest in a nice one?"

She grabbed his shoulders. "Are you serious? You'd really stay here?"

He caressed her hair and held her face between his hands. "Don't make me leave. I've fallen in love with you and I'd hate to part with the children."

"You love me?" She threw her arms around his neck. "Oh, Adam, I love you so much. You're the man I've always dreamed of finding. Yet, you found me."

"I don't plan for us to be apart, not if you'll let me stay." He kissed her.

When they eventually broke apart, he caressed her face. "The kiss we shared at our wedding was sweet temptation. I've dreamed of holding you as your husband ever since. Lying beside you each night but not making love to you has been torture."

"I confess I've thought about that kiss many times. Not turning to you at night has been difficult. You've been such a gentleman, I thought perhaps you didn't desire me and the wedding kiss was just for show."

"From the first evening I met you, I've thought you were the kindest, prettiest, and most perfect woman I'd ever me. Every day has reinforced my opinion."

He stood and took her hand. "Come to our room and let me show you how I feel about you."

"I long to know, Mr. Bennett."

"I'll spend our lifetime showing you."

Epilogue

June 1885

Garnet helped Hyacinth with her new pink dress. When it was fastened, she brushed the little girl's golden curls and anchored a wide pink grosgrain bow.

"There, you look like a real princess."

Hyacinth twirled around her room. "Where are we going?"

"It's a surprise, remember? You'll know soon enough."

Today she'd hired someone to operate the café. Adam and Joey came to the door.

"My, you gentlemen look especially handsome today." Her husband resembled a Norse god. Joey's sandy hair was darker than Adam's, but close enough they could have been father and son.

Adam bowed. "We did our best because we're escorting two beautiful women. Shall we go?"

Joey held Adam's hand. "I like surprises but I sure wish I knew where we were going."

Garnet held Hyacinth's hand as they strolled. "We're heading to the mayor's office?"

Hyacinth tugged on Garnet's hand. "Maybe you got me a pony."

Adam laughed. "No pony, Princess Hyacinth."

Eyes full of question, Joey asked, "What is this about?"

Adam chuckled. "You'll see soon enough."

Joey couldn't stand the mystery. "You never let someone else run the café. Why we're going must be important."

Garnet said, "Very much so."

At the mayor's office, Owen Vaile waited for them behind a desk. "Well, this is a fine looking family. Come in and have a seat."

When they were seated, Owen looked at Joey and Hyacinth. "Children, would you step up to the desk, please?"

GARNET

Both looked at Garnet. She smiled and nodded.

Owen held a sheaf of papers in his hands. "Children I have to interview you to see if this meets with your wishes. Garnet and Adam Bennett have petitioned to adopt you."

Joey glanced over his shoulder with a wide smile before he took his sister's hand. "Did you hear, Hyacinth? Garnet and Adam want to adopt us. That means we'd be theirs forever and no one could take us away from them."

Hyacinth ran to hug Garnet's neck.

"Thank you, dear, but go back and listen to Mr. Vaile."

Owen cleared his throat. "I take it this meets with your approval. Do you agree that you want to be adopted by Garnet and Adam?"

Joey stood very straight. "Yes, sir, I do."

Hyacinth stood beside him.

Joey whispered to her, "You have to say you want to be adopted."

She said, "I want to be 'dopted."

"What name do you wish to use, Chandler or Bennett?"

Joey appeared to think a few seconds. "Can't I use both?"

Owen chuckled. "Yes, I see no reason why you can't be Josiah Chandler Bennett. Is that what you want?"

"Yes, sir. That's perfect."

"Miss Hyacinth, do you want to be Hyacinth Chandler Bennett?"

"If I get to say, I want to be Princess Hyacinth Chandler Bennett."

Garnet and Adam smothered their laughter.

Owen coughed to cover his. "I don't have the power to officially designate you as Princess, but I'll add Bennett to your name. I believe your new parents already treat you as a princess."

"I get new parents? I want to stay with Garnet and Adam."

Owen spoke patiently. "Your Aunt Garnet and Uncle Adam are now your new mother and father because of the adoption."

Hyacinth leaned forward. "Want to know a secret? We're gonna get a baby pretty soon. If you ask, Garnet might let you put a hand on her tummy and feel the baby kick. Can you believe the baby is right there inside her tummy."

Garnet pulled her daughter back to her. "I think Mr. Vaile guessed we're going to get a baby soon." Being seven months pregnant was hard to hide.

Adam paid Owen and received the adoption papers. "Thank you for all your help."

Owen gave a broad smile. "You have your work cut out for you. The four of you make a nice family."

Adam opened the door. "That we do, a large part in thanks to you." He closed the door behind him.

The four of them walked down the street toward the café.

Adam gestured ahead. "How about stopping at the Sugar and Spice Bakery and getting a treat?"

Garnet headed for the bakery. "I'll enjoy the change of being a customer instead of cook."

Adam scooted his chair close to Garnet's. "There'll be more of this kind of outing now that you have part-time staff to step in when you want off."

"I can't help worrying."

"I know, but try. I want us to do things as a family—go on a picnic, go up to Angel Springs, go visit friends."

"Sounds lovely, Adam. I'm so lucky you came to the café when you were hungry."

"I'm grateful you were kind and compassionate. I've found the perfect place to spend my life. I've never been happier."

"I never dreamed anyone could be this happy. If I didn't feel the size of a barn, my life would be perfect."

"You're the most beautiful barn I've ever seen. You can park in my pasture any time you wish."

"Adam Bennett, you say the sweetest things.

GARNET

Dear Reader,

Thank you for choosing to read my book out of the millions available. If you'd like to know about my new releases, contests, giveaways, and other events, please sign up for my reader group at www.carolineclemmons.com. New subscribers receive a *Free* historical western titled *Happy Is The Bride*.

Join me and other readers at **Caroline's Cuties**, a Facebook group at https://www.facebook.com/groups/277082053015947/ for special excerpts, exchanging ideas, contests, giveaways, recipes. and talking to people about books.

If you enjoyed this story, please leave a review wherever you purchased the book. You'll be helping me and prospective readers and I'll appreciate your effort.

Caroline

If you downloaded this book without purchase from a pirating site, please read it with the author's compliments. If you enjoy it, please consider purchasing a legal copy to support the author in writing further books. If you can't afford to buy it, please leave a review on Amazon or Goodreads – it really helps!

Those who prefer reading western historical romance will enjoy being a member of the **Pioneer Hearts Facebook Group**. There you'll be able to converse with authors and readers about books, contests, new releases, and a myriad of other subjects involving western historical romance. Sign up at https://www.facebook.com/groups/pioneerhearts/

CAROLINE CLEMMONS

The Widows Of Wildcat Ridge Series
Sweet western historical romances

Title	Author	Release Date
Priscilla	Charlene Raddon	September 15, 2018
Blessing	Caroline Clemmons	October 1, 2018
Nissa	Zina Abbott	October 15, 2018
Gwyneth	Christine Sterling	November 1, 2018
Dulcina	Linda Caroll-Bradd	November 15, 2018
Josephine	Kit Morgan	November 30, 2018
Thalia	Charlene Raddon	December 15, 2018
Eleanora	Pam Crooks	January 1, 2019
Garnet	Caroline Clemmons	January 15, 2019
Grace	Tracy Garrett	February 1, 2019
Rosemary	Kristy McCaffery	February 15, 2019
Clare	Kit Morgan	March 1, 2019
Cadence	Charlene Raddon	March 15, 2019
Diantha	Zina Abbott	April 1, 2019
Hazelanne	Linda Carroll-Bradd	April 15, 2019
Melanie	Margaret Tanner	May 1, 2019
Ophelia	Charlene Raddon	May 15, 2019

Read Caroline's western historical titles:

Mistletoe Mistake, sweet Christmas story set in Montana

Blessing, Widows of Wildcat Ridge, set in Utah, sweet

Loving A Rancher Series (sweet)
Amanda's Rancher, No. 1
The Rancher and the Shepherdess, No. 2
Murdoch's Bride, No. 3
Bride's Adventure, No. 4
Snare His Heart, No. 5

GARNET

Capture Her Heart, No. 6
Loving A Rancher, No. 7

Patience, Bride of Washington, American Mail-Order Brides Series #42, sweet

Bride Brigade Series: sweet, set in Texas
Josephine, Bride Brigade book 1
Angeline, Bride Brigade book 2
Cassandra, Bride Brigade book 3
Ophelia, Bride Brigade book 4
Rachel, Bride Brigade book 5
Lorraine, Bride Brigade book 6
Prudence, Bride Brigade book 7

The Surprise Brides: Jamie, sensual, released simultaneously with three other of The Surprise Brides books which are: *Gideon* by Cynthia Woolf, *Caleb* by Callie Hutton, and *Ethan* by Sylvia McDaniel, each book is about one of the Fraser brothers of Angel Springs, Colorado

The Kincaid Series: Sensual, set in Texas
The Most Unsuitable Wife, Kincaids book one
The Most Unsuitable Husband, Kincaids book two
The Most Unsuitable Courtship, Kincaids book three
Gabe Kincaid, Kincaids book four

Stone Mountain (Texas) Series:

Brazos Bride, Men of Stone Mountain Texas book one, **Free,** sensual
Buy the Audiobook here
High Stakes Bride, Men of Stone Mountain Texas book two, sensual
Buy the Audiobook here
Bluebonnet Bride, Men of Stone Mountain Texas book three, sensual
Tabitha's Journey, a Stone Mountain Texas mail-order bride novella, sweet

CAROLINE CLEMMONS

Stone Mountain Reunion, a Stone Mountain Texas short story, sweet
Stone Mountain Christmas, a Stone Mountain Texas Christmas novella, sweet
Winter Bride, a Stone Mountain Texas romance, sweet

McClintocks: set in Texas
The Texan's Irish Bride, McClintocks book one, **Free**, sensual
O'Neill's Texas Bride, McClintocks book two, sweet
McClintock's Reluctant Bride, McClintocks book three
Daniel McClintock, McClintocks book four, sweet

Save Your Heart For Me, a mildly sensual romance adventure novella set in Texas

Long Way Home, a sweet-ish Civil War adventure romance set in Georgia

Caroline's Texas Time Travels
Out Of The Blue, 1845 Irish lass comes forward to today Texas, sensual
Texas Lightning, sweet, 1896 woman rancher comes forward to today
Texas Rainbow, sweet, 1920s flapper comes forward to today
Texas Storm, sweet, WWII WASP comes forward to today

Caroline's Contemporary Titles

Angel For Christmas, sweet Christmas tale of second chances, sweet

Texas Caprock Tales:
Be My Guest, mildly sensual with mystery, sensual
Grant Me The Moon, sweet with mystery,

Snowfires, sensual, set in Texas

Home Sweet Texas Home, Texas Home book one, sweet

Caroline's Mysteries: (Texas)

GARNET

Almost Home, a Link Dixon mystery
Death In The Garden, a Heather Cameron cozy mystery

Take Advantage of Bargain Boxed Sets:
Mail-Order Tangle: Linked books: Mail-Order Promise by Caroline Clemmons and Mail-Order Ruckus by Jacquie Rogers, set in Texas and Idaho
Under A Mulberry Moon, nine-author anthology, July 2018, available for a limited time, novellas by Zina Abbott, Patricia Pacjac Carroll, Caroline Clemmons, Carra Copelin, Keta Diablo, P. A. Estelle, Cissie Patterson, Charlene Raddon, and Jacquie Rogers.
Cinderella Treasure Trove, excerpts, blurbs, author bios, and recipes from authors who write books with a new take on a fairy tale. Free
Musings and Medleys, blurbs, excerpts, recipes, and author bios from the authors in Under A Mulberry Moon. Free

CAROLINE CLEMMONS

About Caroline Clemmons

Through a crazy twist of fate, Caroline Clemmons was *not* born on a Texas ranch. To make up for this tragic error, she writes about handsome cowboys, feisty ranch women, and scheming villains in a small office her family calls her pink cave. She and her Hero live in North Central Texas cowboy country where they ride herd on their rescued cats and dogs. The books she creates there have made her an Amazon bestselling author and won several awards. Find her on her **blog**, **website**, **Facebook**, **Twitter**, **Goodreads**, **Google+**, and **Pinterest**.

Click on her **Amazon Author Page** for a complete list of her books and follow her there.

Follow her on **BookBub**.

Subscribe to Caroline's newsletter to receive a FREE novella of HAPPY IS THE BRIDE, a humorous historical wedding disaster that ends happily—but you knew it would, didn't you?

She loves to hear from readers at **caroline@carolineclemmons.com**